Michael Underwood and The Murder Room

>>> This title is part of The Murder Room, our series dedicated to making available out-of-print or hard-to-find titles by classic crime writers.

Crime fiction has always held up a mirror to society. The Victorians were fascinated by sensational murder and the emerging science of detection; now we are obsessed with the forensic detail of violent death. And no other genre has so captivated and enthralled readers.

Vast troves of classic crime writing have for a long time been unavailable to all but the most dedicated frequenters of second-hand bookshops. The advent of digital publishing means that we are now able to bring you the backlists of a huge range of titles by classic and contemporary crime writers, some of which have been out of print for decades.

From the genteel amateur private eyes of the Golden Age and the femmes fatales of pulp fiction, to the morally ambiguous hard-boiled detectives of mid twentieth-century America and their descendants who walk our twenty-first century streets, The Murder Room has it all. **>>>**

The Murder Room
Where Criminal Minds Meet

themurderroom.com

Michael Underwood (1916–1992)

Michael Underwood (the pseudonym of John Michael Evelyn) was born in Worthing, Sussex and educated at Christ Church College, Oxford. He was called to the Bar in 1939 and served in the British army during World War Two. He returned to work in the Department of Public Prosecutions until his retirement in 1976, and wrote almost 50 crime novels informed by his career in the law. His five series characters include Sergeant Nick Atwell and lawyer Rosa Epton, of whom is was said by the *Washington Post* that she 'outdoes Perry Mason'.

The Man Who Died on Friday

Michael Underwood

An Orion book

Copyright © Isobel Mackenzie 1967

The right of Michael Underwood to be identified as the author of this work has been asserted in accordance with the Copyright, Designs and Patents Act 1988.

This edition published by
The Orion Publishing Group Ltd
Orion House
5 Upper St Martin's Lane
London WC2H 9EA

An Hachette UK company
A CIP catalogue record for this book is available from the British Library

ISBN 978 1 4719 0822 4

www.orionbooks.co.uk

To Michael Legat

Just occasionally London presents a splendidly washed appearance. It always follows a period of heavy rain and high winds and lasts only a few hours. Then the diesel fumes and the smoke reassert themselves and a gauze of smog once more settles over the Metropolis. This pearl of a moment is best caught in the early evening when the lights have come on and dance in reflection across every shining pavement and up every glistening wall, and when, too, the tops of the buildings stand silhouetted against the subdued glow of the sky's perimeter.

Such an evening was Friday, March 4th, and though Joseph Berg had other, and more anxious, matters to occupy his mind, he paused to take brief notice of its beauty. If anyone had happened to be with him, he would most probably have commented on the city's feat in managing to look, and above all to smell, clean.

The street in which he had parked was off the Fulham Road and about a quarter of a mile from his destination. It had been impressed upon him that he shouldn't leave the car any closer than this. He carefully locked the driver's door and walked round trying the others. Then, because he was nervous, he went round and tried them a second time. The street was lined on both sides by an assortment of ageing vehicles, some of them covered over with protective sheets and looking like ill-wrapped parcels which gave his 1963 Jaguar the appearance of being on a slumming expedition.

Though he wasn't cold, Berg turned up his mackintosh collar and withdrew his head like a wary tortoise. He was a short, dark man of unmemorable appearance in his early forties, but his nervousness made him feel nakedly conspicuous. He wished, not for the first time, that he had never got drawn into these crazy cloak and dagger activities. They caused great personal inconvenience and, worse, considerable nervous strain. The trouble was that, having once weakly consented to play a minor role, it had become almost impossible to back out. Not, in his case, because of any threat of blackmail, but because of the blatant appeal to loyalty, with the subtle, unfair suggestion that his philosophy was no better than the I'm-all-right-Jack variety whenever he had demurred and asked them to find someone else to run their errands.

As he walked away from the car, the briskness of his step belied the tension which flowed out of his nerve-ends, but he looked determinedly ahead and glanced neither to right nor left. Not that anyone evinced the slightest interest in him either. He tried focusing his mind on everyday normality: on his home in Hendon where his wife, Hilda, would at this moment be sitting in front of a nice fire watching television, believing her husband to be meeting a business associate—which, in a sense, he was.

"Don't wait up for me, dear," he had said when he left after supper. "I ought to be home by eleven, but you never know on these occasions."

And Hilda had merely nodded. She had long ceased to question her husband's comings and goings. He provided her with all she wanted and her life was complete. And if the truth were told, it was very little less complete when he wasn't there. She had no interest in his business, an export/import agency with offices off Aldgate, and he found little pleasure in her circle of coffee-drinking, bridge-playing friends. Their marriage had reached the stage where each tolerated the other and made the adjustments required by two people living under the same roof, but beyond that their life together was a well which had dried up. He sometimes wondered whether it would have been different had they been able to have children. As it was, he was thankful that there weren't any.

Still thinking in an inconclusive sort of way about Hilda, he turned into Starforth Street which, at a quarter to ten on a Friday evening, was almost empty, though traffic could be seen passing to and fro along the main road at the end, and sounds of singing and of a piano being strummed came from the pub on the corner. Berg walked fifteen or twenty yards towards the lights at the end, then paused and pretended to study the house numbers. A taxi turned into the street from the main road and came toward him with headlights on. He quickly turned his back on it and began to walk rapidly in the direction from which he had come. It passed him and turned left, disappearing from his view. He crossed over to the other side and stood against the wall of a school playground in the flickering shadows cast between two lamp posts. Everything glistened as though it had been coated with glycerine.

He looked at his watch and saw that it was still two minutes to the quarter hour.

From the street plan which he had studied he knew that a minor road ran behind the pub and intersected Starforth Street just short of its junction with the main road. Suddenly, as he now stood peering in that direction, he saw his contact emerge from the shadows and stand for a few seconds outside the lighted saloon bar entrance. He must have been forty or fifty yards from Berg who saw him cast a quick glance his way. Then he crossed to the other side.

Almost immediately he was joined by another figure. They appeared to be speaking, but the only sound was that emanating from the pub. Berg watched intently, realising too late that he ought to have moved closer.

His contact seemed suddenly to slip on the wet pavement and his companion put out a hand. The next second, however, he had slithered to the ground and the man with him had vanished. One moment there; gone the next.

Berg dashed toward the spot where the fallen man lay. He felt his face going stiff with horror as he gazed at the gash in the throat through which the man's life-blood was now being methodically pumped into the gutter. Quickly he turned and ran. As he did so, there was an eruption of noise from the pub opposite. He had almost reached the far end of the street before there was a shout behind him.

"Hi, you. Stop!" But Joseph Berg continued to run.

Richard Monk was a young man with a thoroughly healthy attitude toward work, best evidenced, perhaps, by the zest and eagerness with which he returned to his office each Monday morning. Not that he found his weekends boring; on the contrary, he enjoyed them very much. It was just that he found being a solicitor an absorbing occupation. And those of his profession who didn't share this enthusiasm might have been more inclined to do so if they, too, had been their own masters and had a pleasant office in Bedford Square from which to conduct their business.

As he mounted the two steps to the front entrance, he glanced with self-conscious pride at the brass plate with the legend,

Richard Monk & Co.
Solicitors and Commissioners for Oaths.

It shone, even under the leaden sky of promised snow.

"'Morning, Roy," he called out as he passed the open door of his assistant. Though Roy Harding was a few years older than Richard, he was only a salaried partner and also the only other legally qualified member of the firm. However, it was his name appearing on the letter-head which justified the "& Co."

"Hello, Richard. Have a good weekend?"

"Terrific. I went sailing."

"At this time of year?"

"It was a bit chilly."

"Must have been for you to notice." Richard grinned and Harding went on, "Incidentally, Richard, I shall be out most of the day. That probate action starts today."

"Splendid probate weather. Now it's certain to snow. How long'll it last?"

"A day and a half at most."

Richard looked thoughtful. "That's long enough for you to be out of the office at one go. We really ought to discuss the need to have an assistant solicitor on your side of the business. We don't want to turn away any of the bread and butter work."

It was his habit to refer to the conveyancing, the will-making and the divorce work as the bread and butter stuff and to his own criminal work as the boss's hobby. And this, in a sense, was true, as all too often his own cases brought little by way of financial reward. But then if you'd been left £400,000 at the age of twenty-eight (he was now thirty-one) you could afford to indulge yourself by not regarding the acquisition of further money as a main object in life. Not that Richard Monk & Co. was an insolvent concern. Quite the reverse, though this was not due to its principal's earning capacity.

"Roper and Bentley manage very well," Harding said.

"Oh, I know. They're bloody good clerks, but I'm not sure the moment hasn't arrived to take in another qualified chap. Anyhow, let's talk about it later in the week."

He went upstairs to his own office to find Sheila Gillam, his secretary, hovering in the doorway between their two rooms.

"Good morning, Sheila."

"Good morning, Mr. Monk. I hope you had a nice weekend."

"Very nice." He gave her an enquiring glance as she continued to hover. "You're not looking your usual everything-under-control self, Sheila. Anything up?"

"Only that a Mr. Berg has 'phoned three times in the last half-hour."

He frowned. "I don't know any Mr. Berg, do I?"

"No. And he refused to say what it was about, but he sounded terribly worried."

"What have you done about him?"

"Nothing. I imagine he'll ring again any minute. Will you speak to him when he does?"

"Surely."

Sheila Gillam withdrew and Richard ran a hand through his thatch of always slightly disordered hair and then held a finger to his nose. "Still reeks of the English Channel," he murmured to himself as he sat down at his desk to go through the mail. He was insistent on this ritual, though most of the letters required the attention of Roy Harding or of the two clerks who handled much of the routine work or of the cashier, who resembled a chapel elder. Richard was by training, if not by nature, suspicious of anyone who looked quite as upright and severely virtuous as Mr. Blenkyn, and would never be entirely taken by surprise to learn that he embezzled on the side.

After informing himself on what his employees were up to, he picked up *The Times* to see what had happened in the world since he had last looked at a newspaper. Unlike most people who have a favourite starting point in their morning read, Richard Monk always began on the left hand side of page one and methodically worked his way through to the end. This didn't mean that he absorbed the lot, but his eye did at least slide up and down and across each page and, like a bee seeking pollen, settle on those items of particular interest to him.

He had progressed through "Sports News" and "The Arts" and was approaching the leader page when an item of "Home News" claimed his attention. He read:

Murdered Civil Servant

Police enquiries continue into the murder of Mr. Frederick Parsons, aged 53, a scientific officer in the Ministry of Defence, who was found dying of a stab wound of the throat in Starforth Street, Fulham, last Friday night. Mr. Parsons, who never regained consciousness, died in the ambulance on his way to hospital. A Scotland Yard spokesman said that a motive for the crime had not yet been established. Mr. Parsons lived in Hendon and was married.

The thing which interested Richard was that, not only had no one been charged with the offence, but there wasn't even a description of someone who the police believed might be able to help them with their enquiries. The hand which had struck down Mr. Parsons was disembodied for all the police appeared to know.

Crime had always fascinated him; and the greater the element of mystery, the greater the fascination. The trouble was that real crime seldom achieved the same level of mystery as fictional crime, so that a study of both forms was necessary to bring him full satisfaction.

With his mind still lingering over Mr. Parsons' fate, he skipped through the Prime Minister's latest speech on economic recovery, a long leader on the future of Britain as a maritime nation and a turgid letter from a member of the House of Lords on the need for severer penalties against those he labelled "juvenile delinquent hooligans". Richard fell to wondering if these were the same as "delinquent hooligan juveniles" or "hooligan juvenile delinquents". There seemed no end to the permutations.

He had just finished the paper (crosswords were not *his* addiction) when Sheila came in, bringing him a cup of coffee.

"No further word from Mr. Berg?" he enquired, as she placed the saucer on a piece of blotting paper so that it wouldn't mark the desk.

"No."

"I hope he hasn't thrown himself off Waterloo Bridge."

"Waterloo?" Her tone was surprised.

"Well, any bridge."

"I don't expect he has," she said after a thoughtful pause. "Not many men do."

She was a placid girl, which was as well seeing that she was married to an extremely volatile actor who was subject to fits of black depression. Richard thought she probably regarded him as her yardstick for measuring male instability. If Harold Gillam could keep away from bridges, so could Mr. Berg, however worried he may have sounded.

She withdrew and he picked up his coffee and blew on it hard. It always came hotter than molten steel, and then by the time it was drinkable a great wrinkled layer of skin had formed on top. But, being the boss, he was at least provided with a spoon to remove the skin and a saucer into which to deposit it. He took a sip and quickly licked his scalded lips.

There was a discreet buzz at his left elbow and he lifted the receiver.

"Mr. Berg is in the waiting-room," Sheila announced drily.

"Have you seen him?"

"I've just come up from speaking to him. I told him I had no idea whether you'd be able to see him as you were very busy and normally didn't see anyone without an appointment."

"And what was his reaction to those cooling words of welcome?"

"He said he'd take a chance on your becoming free and be able to see him." After a pause she added, "I don't think he's actually brought sandwiches with him so you could probably starve him off the premises."

"How did he strike you, Sheila?"

"Quiet, but determined."

"Count up to a hundred and then have him sent up. Oh, and

Sheila, you'd better take my cup. I'll drink it this afternoon, it'll be cool by then."

While he was waiting for his visitor, he took a fat pad of thick, creamy paper from his desk drawer and selected a freshly-sharpened pencil from the Benares brass pot which sprouted a dozen or more of different colours. He had a fetish about stationery. Notes written on scraps of paper maddened him, and used envelopes with economy labels even more so. To him a stationer's was the equivalent of Cartiers to a jewel-conscious woman.

There was a soft knock on the door and Sheila opened it.

"Mr. Berg, Mr. Monk," she said, and closed the door as soon as Berg had stepped inside the room. The two men looked at each other.

"I'm very grateful to you for seeing me. I realise I ought to have made an appointment. In fact, as your secretary may have told you, I did ring, but you hadn't come in. So I decided not to waste more time and to take a chance that you'd see me." He brought out his wallet. "Let me give you my card."

He made this little speech from just inside the door, while Richard remained standing at the side of his desk. He now came across the room and shook hands, looking about him with nervous interest.

"If I may say so, it's somewhat different from what I had expected," he said with a flicker of a smile, as Richard glanced at the card which bore Berg's name and address. "Your room, I mean." He observed Richard's puzzled expression. "I'd expected something very modern. A single abstract painting on the wall and a fitted carpet as spongy as Irish moss. That sort of thing."

"That's what I'd have if I were in advertising, but solicitors ought to be traditional. After all, the great mass of the public still associates us with Victorianism." He glanced round his room. "And anyway I happen to be rather fond of early Victoriana—in the right place." He didn't point out the absence of anything Victorian about his attire. A medium grey flannel suit, a coloured shirt with button-down collar, a knitted silk tie and suede shoes (his regular office garb) would have made a Victorian solicitor swallow his quill.

"And especially when it's all the real thing...," Berg murmured, his eyes taking in the mahogany desk with its dark green leather top, the brass table lamp on it and the spread of Turkey carpet beneath it. He looked across at the wall. "Are those originals?"

"The Spy cartoons? No, reproduction of the period."

Berg went across and examined one of them, an iron-faced judge in scarlet and ermine.

"I shouldn't like to have come up in front of him. I hope his sort is not still around."

"May I suggest, Mr. Berg, that you come and sit down and tell me what's brought you to see me?"

Berg nodded slowly and let out an imperceptible sigh. It seemed as if he had been hoping to stall off this moment of explanation. Richard recognised the symptoms, which were the same as those exhibited by the person who goes to the doctor and then hesitates to tell him what is wrong. He knew that clients often became coyly reticent when faced by the actuality of confession.

However, Berg now sat down on the chair at the side of the desk. At first gingerly on the edge, then, since this was too uncomfortable a posture to maintain, he was forced to surrender himself to its capacious embrace. It was the perfect chair for nervous clients, low and deep and as difficult to get out of as a bear pit. He was aware of Richard gazing at him with concentrated interest from somewhere up above.

"Cigarette?" Richard handed him the silver box and Berg took a Turkish. "I don't," he explained as he let the lid fall back. "Well, now?"

There was a silence before Berg said in a voice tight with emotion: "I believe I may be suspected of murder. The murder of a man called Parsons."

"The Ministry of Defence official?"

"That's right. You've read all about it then?" He sounded immeasurably relieved as though any further explanation had become superfluous.

"I've read what's in today's *Times*, but that's not very much. It didn't appear from that as if the police were on to anyone. What makes you think you may be under suspicion?"

"Because somebody intends I should be," Berg said emotionally. "Somebody called Gamel."

"Who's Gamel?"

"He's the man who did murder Parsons."

Monk made a brief note on the pad in front of him and said: "In a moment, I'll want you to tell me the whole story, but first I'd like to ask you a few questions. Just to establish some basic facts. How do you know Gamel killed Parsons?"

"I can only answer that, Mr. Monk, by telling you the whole story."

"All right, then answer me this instead. Where were you when the murder was committed?"

"In Starforth Street. I saw it happen, except that I didn't know at the time I was witnessing a murder. I was about fifty yards away."

"And you recognised this man Gamel?"

"I know it was Gamel because he was the man Parsons went to meet."

"Do you know where Gamel is now?"

Berg shook his head forlornly. "But surely the police will be able to find him? They must find him."

"That depends how hard they look for him," Richard replied and observed Berg wince. "Assuming you're right about Gamel wanting to throw suspicion on you, how can he achieve this?"

"By somehow letting the police know that I was at the scene," Berg said vaguely.

"You've just told me yourself that you were there."

"But the police don't know that."

Richard tried to hide his rising exasperation, but he was always irked by clients who seemed to take it for granted that they could tell him one thing and later expect his support in putting forward a completely different story—in Court for example. Less reputable members of his profession might invent defences for their clients which bore little relation to the given facts, but Richard resented the assumption that he would be prepared to lend himself to this dubious sort of practice. However, to be fair, Berg hadn't yet gone that far, nor indeed had Richard made up his mind definitely to represent him.

"Have the police been to see you?"

"Yes, on Saturday," Berg said uneasily.

"Oh! How did they get on to you?"

Berg stubbed his cigarette out with slow deliberation as though to gain time before answering this question.

"They found my telephone number in Parsons' diary."

"I don't suppose it was the only one. Was that all?"

"I'm afraid not. Against last Friday's date there was my name and beside it 'The Duchess of Bedford, 10 o'clock.' "

"Where's the Duchess of Bedford?"

"It's the pub on the corner of Starforth Street."

"Were these diary entries in Parsons' writing?"

"I assume so. They weren't in mine. I didn't even know he had a diary."

"Was there any reference to Gamel in the diary?"

"I don't know. The police didn't say anything about him."

"Did you mention him to them?"

"No, I thought it better not to."

"Did you tell them you'd been in Starforth Street last Friday night?"

Berg seemed to shrink as he hung his head and said miserably: "I'm afraid I told them that I hadn't been there. I told them I didn't know why Parsons had made such an entry in his diary . . . their visit was all so unexpected and I didn't have time to think straight . . . I told them a stupid lie."

Richard reflected that the degree of its stupidity would depend upon the ease with which it could be shown up.

He said: "I haven't asked you this, but I gather you did know the dead man?"

"Yes, although not particularly well. He lived in the next street to mine and we'd met socially a few times."

"How long had you known him?"

"Four or five years."

"Did you tell the police that?"

"Oh, yes. I never pretended I didn't know him." He seemed to find relief in this admission of truth. But it was short-lived.

"Did the police ask you where you were on Friday night?"

"I told them I'd gone to meet a business client, but that he failed to turn up."

Richard silently groaned. How often he'd heard it all before, the small initial lie, leading to more lies and finally the runaway cancer of lies.

"I suppose they asked you for the name of your client?"

"Yes."

"And what'll he say when the police make a cross-check?"

Berg shrugged helplessly. "I don't know. I haven't been able to get in touch with him. I realise I'm in an awful mess."

"And did you tell them where you were going to meet this client?" Richard went on remorselessly.

"I had to. I mentioned a public house in Mayfair I've been to a few times."

"Can anyone prove you never set foot inside the place last Friday evening?"

"I don't know. It's always pretty full and I'm not a regular. The staff probably wouldn't notice whether I was there or not."

"But the police will certainly check on that too," Richard remarked bleakly. "Did they make it clear that they regarded you as being under suspicion?"

"They were perfectly polite, but at the same time very tenacious in their questioning. When they left they said they would certainly want to see me again."

"But so far, they haven't?"

"Not yet."

"Incidentally, what was the name of the officer?"

"Detective-Inspector Evans. I think he said he was from Fulham Police Station."

Richard tore a page from his notepad and tapped his teeth lightly with his pencil. Then looking up suddenly he said: "And now finally before you give me the full background to what you've already told me, I'd like to ask how you come to consult *me*?"

"I remembered your name from a newspaper article. It was after you'd successfully defended that police officer who'd been framed."

Richard nodded. He remembered the article all too well. It portrayed him as a quixotic defender of the oppressed who was ready to spend his own money in the attainment of justice for his clients. The result had been off-stage sounds of displeasure from the Law Society and, worse, an absolute flood of importunate demands from every crank and crook in the country.

"If I may say so, Mr. Monk, it made you sound a rather remarkable person. I don't wish to embarrass you, but it mentioned qualities which are all too rare nowadays; at least in my line of business, where it's every man grab for himself and survival of the fittest. The article I read made it appear that your standards were less materialistic than most people's." He paused and said awkwardly, "I apologise if I've embarrassed you, but I was only trying to answer your question. Perhaps I ought to add quickly that I haven't come to you with my begging bowl outstretched. I mayn't be a millionaire, but I certainly can afford to pay a lawyer's fees. I wouldn't want you to think that because I mentioned that article I was hoping to receive free advice."

"Let's forget the article," Richard said firmly. Then with a small smile of encouragement he went on, "Now tell me what led up to your being in Starforth Street last Friday night."

Berg played nervously with his fingers for a while, as though trying to make sure they were properly jointed, before addressing his opening remarks to the patch of carpet between his legs.

"It all stems from the fact that I'm a Jew," he said slowly. "Not a strict one from the point of view of religious observance, but still a Jew. Both my parents were Jews and I have most of the feelings of blood ties which bind Jews together. Perhaps I should mention that I was born and educated in this country and I served in the army in the latter stages of the war. So you can see I'm one of those very British Jews."

"What's your business?"

"I run an import/export agency. I started it up in 1950 and it's been quite successful. I have about twenty or thirty employees. We do business with a lot of continental firms, as well as with a few in America, and I also have connections with Israel. Moreover, I have a brother there. He left this country in 1934 when he was twenty and he's lived in Israel ever since."

"And he is now one of your business connections?"

"Not exactly. You see, he's a painter, though he does come into the story. As a matter of fact between 1934 and 1955 I never saw him, but during the past twelve years I've been to Israel five or six times and we've usually met. We're not particularly close. I was only eleven or twelve when he left England and so our lives developed quite separately. I mention all this because I think it's important that you should understand the exact nature of our relationship."

"The ties of blood remain even though any personal common interest has died with the years."

"Precisely, Mr. Monk. Now let me tell you about Parsons—or as much about him as I know. Soon after I first met him I realised from remarks he let drop that he was violently anti-Arab. Later I learnt that his younger brother, to whom he'd apparently been devoted, had been killed in the army at the time of Suez. When I say killed, I mean tortured and murdered."

"Where did that happen?"

"In Alexandria."

"And that was the reason for his anti-Arab sentiments?"

"Yes. It was more than that, it was a slow, smouldering hatred. A determination to do them down in any way he could. I suppose because he knew I was a Jew, he expressed himself rather more freely in my presence than he did in other people's. Not that he told me all this at one time. It came out in bits and pieces over a period." Berg moistened his lips with his tongue and went on, "But the real bolt from the blue came only nine months ago. We had met at a local cocktail party and afterwards he and his wife came back for coffee with us. The women went into the house and he came with me when I went to put the car away. Quite suddenly—I can remember it clearly, I had just locked the garage door—he said, 'I have some information which would interest the Israel government, I think. You could be the person to pass it on to them.' I looked at him in astonishment for a minute before I said, 'You must be out of your mind talking like that. People go to prison for twenty-five years and more for spying.' I was even more astonished when he let out a laugh. 'This is not spying. At least not in the sense you mean. Anyway, let me tell you about it.' " Berg glanced up at Richard and said ruefully, "And like a fool, I let him. We must have stood there in the shadow of the garage for nearly half an hour. I know we had to make some excuse about the lock jamming when we eventually got into the house. Stripped of its detail, his story was this. That about a year before, he had hit upon the idea of offering himself to the Arabs as a spy with the intention all the time of feeding them false information. His job in the Ministry gave him access to a certain amount of secret technical data in the weapon research field and he had been supplying this after, as he put it, scrambling it a bit first. Altering figures and that sort of thing. Enough, I gathered, to make it valueless but not enough for it to be apparent. Anyway, he was highly delighted with his little scheme and he told me how they'd fallen for it hook, line and sinker, believing that they'd seduced an important official in the

Ministry of Defence. He even managed to be amused by the money he received. It wasn't very much, but used to send it to a Zionist charity and this gave him the most satisfaction of all."

"Was he a Jew?"

"No. It was just that selling worthless information to the Arabs and giving the money to their arch enemies was, to him, the most exquisite form of revenge he could devise for what they'd done to his brother."

Richard made a face. "He doesn't sound a very normal sort of man."

"No one who harbours that amount of hatred can be normal. I only wish I'd seen all this as clearly at the beginning as I do now. Anyway his suggestion was that I should, through my business contacts, let the Israel government know what he was doing."

"You mean, he would let you have details of the false information he was passing to the Arabs?"

"Yes. It was just a further refinement in his extraction of revenge. At the time I was non-committal, though I made up my mind to sound out my brother when I went to Israel about two weeks later. Parsons knew I was due to make a visit as I'd been talking about it at the party. Well, I did mention it to my brother and, to cut a longish story short, before I left Israel I was given full instructions how to transmit the information. Quite frankly, I was rather taken aback. I hadn't expected such a prompt and positive reaction. But from that moment there was no turning back. When I returned to England, I got in touch with Parsons and told him I would co-operate with him."

"Just before you go on, I'm not quite clear about the people you saw in Israel. Were your dealings in the matter solely with your brother?"

"I first mentioned the matter to my brother, and the next day he telephoned me at my hotel in Haifa and told me to expect a visit that evening from a Mr. Malmed. Mr. Malmed had obviously been told the whole story before he came, because all he did was to instruct me in channels of communication. I was simply to pass the information in an envelope marked 'Invoice' to the Shraga Shipping Company of Haifa. He told me I didn't need to know anything else and merely added something about it being the duty of every Jew everywhere to play his part in safeguarding the national home."

"Did you gather who he was?"

"I assumed he was a member of the Israel Security Service. He didn't say so, of course, but he had that sort of quiet alertness about him that cloak and dagger operators seem to acquire."

Richard thought of the only person he knew in this particular field and decided that it was an apt description.

"And so it began," Berg said wearily. "About once a month, I'd meet Parsons by arrangement, he'd hand me some documents and within twenty-four hours they'd be on their way to Haifa."

"Did you ever hear anything further from that end?"

Berg shook his head. "And the last time I was in Israel, I didn't see my brother. He was away somewhere and I was unable to get in touch with him."

"So as far as you're concerned, you've just been sending things off into the void?"

"Yes. I imagine I would have heard from them, if nothing had been received."

"Were you paid for your services?"

"No. It was never suggested, and they took it for granted that I was doing it as a patriotic duty."

There was a tinge of resentment in his tone which was not lost on Richard.

"Well, weren't you?"

"As I explained earlier, Mr. Monk, I may be a hundred percent Jewish, but England is my home land and I have never acted against the interests of this country, not even during the pre-independence troubles when a good many Jews here found themselves being pulled in two directions. I know my brother who fought bitterly against the British at that time regards me with reservation as a result. He was a member of what here would have been called one of the Zionist terror organisations. They stabbed and killed British soldiers at every opportunity. They were the heroes of their own country, but callous assassins in the eyes of people here. To be a Jew in England in the late forties was a schizophrenic experience and not one to be envied. But to come back to your question, yes, I was acting out of a sense of patriotic duty—perhaps I was even trying to redeem my con-science for earlier neglect—but it wasn't a patriotic duty so fer-vently felt that I didn't slightly resent it being taken for granted, which it undoubtedly was by my brother and Mr. Malmed and the unknowns in the background." He gave Richard a wisp of a smile. "I'm sorry. There's no one more tedious than the Jew who analyses his motives aloud in the hope of achieving self-justification. Where had I got to?"

"I think you were probably about to tell me about Friday night."

Berg nodded abstractedly, as he plucked at his left eyebrow. A hair came away and he examined it thoughtfully before flicking it off his finger.

"About a month ago Parsons told me that he was a bit worried about Gamel as he thought he might have begun to suspect a double-cross. He didn't give me any reason, but he asked me to be somewhere in the vicinity the next time he was due to meet Gamel and pass him something. That meeting was fixed for a quarter to ten last Friday evening in Starforth Street, and it was arranged that I should keep him and Gamel under observation and that at ten o'clock we should meet in the Duchess of Bedford. And that's why I was in Starforth Street, and how I came to be a witness to Parsons' death."

He lay back in the chair, exhausted by his narration of events. Then like a patient hanging on the doctor's word he turned his gaze eagerly toward Richard.

"What do you think?"

"Think?"

"Of my chances?"

"When the police find out that you lied to them about your movements on Friday evening, they'll certainly scrutinise the evidence extremely closely to see whether they have enough to charge you. As far as you know, did anyone see you at the scene?"

"I don't think so. But how can they have enough if I didn't do it?"

"Much'll depend on whether they can establish a motive of any sort. For example if they find out that you and Parsons have been involved in the activities you've been describing to me, I think you must expect to be charged." He observed Berg's defeated expression and added, "But there's a lot of difference between being charged and being convicted, so don't despair. But I always believe in telling clients the worst if I think they can take it."

"Thank you," Berg said quietly, "I appreciate your candour. I can see that the most vital task is to find Gamel. He must be found." His voice broke slightly as he went on, "Gamel is the one person who can save me."

"Maybe, but don't overlook that it's not in his interest to save you. He can only save you by incriminating himself, and he's not likely to do that voluntarily. But I agree that he must be found. Tell me something about him? What nationality is he? What's he doing in this country?"

"He's an Egyptian student at London University. I believe he has lodgings somewhere in the Fulham-Hammersmith area."

"Presumably, then, he must be on the aliens register and we shall be able to trace him through that. Or rather the police will if we put them up to it."

"Provided Gamel is his real name."

"Any reason for thinking otherwise?"

"Except that I understood from Parsons that his student pose was a front for spying activities, in which case Gamel might only be a cover name."

"Hmm. Well, we can but try. Did Parsons tell you how he came to contact Gamel in the first place?"

Berg shook his head. "And I never asked him. I thought the less I knew, the better. I never even examined the documents he gave me. I simply acted as a post office."

"And you never met Gamel?"

"I've never had anything to do with him. All I know is that Parsons once told me that he resembled a surprised horse."

"Not, from that description, the faceless man in the crowd," Richard observed drily. "Can you describe him at all from what you saw of him on Friday?"

"I'm afraid not. He was just a figure. I wouldn't even have recognised Parsons but for his unusual gait."

Richard made a further note and looked over what he had written so far.

"Except for Parsons, did anyone know you were engaged in these activites?"

"No one in this country."

"Your wife didn't know?"

"No."

"And no one in your office had any idea what you were up to?"

18

Again he shook his head. "No, not a soul."

Richard leant forward, resting his cupped hands on the edge of the desk. "That seems to be as far as we can go at the moment, Mr. Berg. My advice to you is short. Don't say anything more to the police. When they get in touch with you again, tell them that I'm your legal representative and that you don't wish to say anything without my being present. I'll then decide whether it's in your interest to say anything."

"Are they likely to accept that?"

"Yes."

"I mean, one reads of people being arrested and not being allowed to get in touch with their lawyers until the police have finished questioning them and that sort of thing."

"In selected cases, maybe," Richard said sardonically, "but it won't happen here."

"And what do I do in the meantime?"

"Carry on as if nothing had happened. It's possible that nothing further will." Though Richard privately doubted this.

After Sheila had shown Berg out, Richard walked across to one of the two full-length windows and looked out into the square. He thought about the story he had just been told and decided it was probably the truth as far as it went. Clients invariably held back something, not in order to mislead deliberately, but out of shame or embarrassment, and in the pathetic wish to preserve at least one protective skin, though all the others have been peeled away.

He heard the front door close and a second later saw Berg step on to the pavement and walk off in the direction of Tottenham Court Road, a hunched and lonely figure. He was about to turn away when his attention was drawn to a young man in a raincoat moving quickly toward a small grey mini-van. He got into the driving seat and it pulled away in the direction Berg had taken.

There was nothing very remarkable in this, save that Richard felt sure the young man had been loitering rather aimlessly at the corner of the square when he'd first become aware of him and secondly that the van had been parked at a place which normally brought traffic wardens hurrying up like wasps to a jam feast. And there was a warden about. He could see him now. He must have walked right past the van only a few minutes ago.

He returned to his desk and rang for Sheila.

"Did you notice anyone keeping us under observation while Mr. Berg was here?" he asked.

"Do you mean that grey van?"

"Could be."

"I couldn't think why the warden let it stay there all that time. Particularly as it's Harrying Harry on duty this morning."

"Did you notice the young man with the van?"

"No. I just happened to look out of the window as Harrying Harry was passing it, and instead of acting as if he's uncovered a plot to blow up Bedford Square he strolled by like a tom-cat with its tail in the air."

"Interesting. Police trailing him, at a guess," Richard murmured, and set about dictating a note on Berg's visit. When he had finished, Sheila closed her shorthand book and put her chair back against the wall. Early on she had refused to take shorthand sitting in the visitors' chair. "Easier to take it upside down in a barrel," she had observed.

"There's something funny about that man," she said as she prepared to return to her own room.

"In what way?"

"Doing all that without ever giving his wife a hint of what he was up to."

"Speaking as a bachelor, it doesn't strike me as being all that unusual."

"Speaking as a married woman, it does me."

"But, Sheila, the wives of spies are not let into their husbands' secrets. If they were, the nations' secrets would soon be flowing through the salons of every hairdresser in the world."

"What nonsense! And, anyway, I'm not saying they'd tell their wives all the details of their work, but I'm certain the wives would know what their husbands did in a general way. And if they didn't, then there'd be something wrong with the marriage."

Richard shrugged. "I don't see how you can generalise."

"You'll see!" Sheila retorted, and closed the door behind her.

Richard made a wry face at the empty room. Sheila was a good secretary and a nice girl, though she wouldn't be his choice for a wife. If she didn't actually wear the trousers, she would have at least one leg in them.

At about twenty to one, he put through a call to Alan Scarby at his chambers. The clerk answered and told him Alan had just gone across to hall for lunch as he had a one-thirty summons before one of the Masters. Richard said he'd try again in the course of the afternoon and assured the clerk that it was nothing urgent. But the fear of losing a thousand-guinea brief by a misplaced word was a morbid reality amongst barristers' clerks when speaking to solicitors, and Alan's was no exception, even though he knew the two men were old friends.

"I could easily send over for him, Mr. Monk," he said.

"Good heavens, no."

"I'll certainly see that he calls you as soon as he gets back to chambers."

"That'll be fine."

Richard Monk and Alan Scarby had been close friends since they'd arrived at school as new boys together. It had been one of the lesser-known public schools which Richard's guardian (his parents had been killed in a car accident when he was only three years old) had chosen because the fees were lower than anywhere else. When each of them left at the age of eighteen, Scarby had gone on to Oxford, but the guardian had vetoed Richard's hope of also going to university and had articled him to a firm of solicitors, with the admonition that the sooner he earned his own living the better. The result was that he was fully qualified at the age of twenty-three and five years later his guardian died suddenly of a brain haemorrhage, leaving him a fortune. Uncle Arthur—the guardian—a gruff, lifelong misogynist had never so much as dropped a hint that Richard was his heir and, having regard to his outspoken views on young men with too much money, Richard had given the prospects little thought. Moreover, there had been nothing about Uncle Arthur's way of life to suggest that he was an extremely wealthy man.

In the event his death brought about a curious reversal in the respective positions of Richard and his friend. Richard became overnight an almost disgustingly rich young bachelor at the same time as Alan, a struggling young member of the Bar, acquired a wife and, nine months later, a daughter.

Their friendship had, however, comfortably survived these vicissitudes and, in addition, Richard, the solicitor, now frequently briefed Alan, the barrister. They had, indeed, been professionally associated in the case of the framed police officer to which Berg had made reference. If Alan Scarby had wistful moments when he envied his friend all the blessings which flow from an absence of any financial worries, Richard, for his part, had always admired Alan for his fluency and easy charm. The one was a romantic adventurer manqué, the other a sophisticated conformist.

Richard strolled across to the window, studied the sky and decided to go out to lunch himself, which meant a cup of coffee and a slice of pizza at a place round the corner. He never ate much in the middle of the day.

"I'm going out now, Sheila," he said, peering round the door into the small room she occupied.

There was a flask of coffee beside her typewritter, on which was propped a magazine, and a lettuce sandwich was half-way to her mouth.

"I'm terribly sorry, Mr. Monk," she gasped. "I thought I heard you go out five minutes ago, or I wouldn't have begun eating. I feel as bad as if you'd caught me with my hair in curlers."

He looked at her in mild surprise. As far as he was concerned it was quite reasonable for her to have started her lunch. As long as she didn't come dropping crumbs over his desk, he didn't mind how often, or when, she consumed snacks in her own domain.

"Don't apologise to me, Sheila," he said. "I didn't even mind when you found me with my socks off."

"That's an employer's prerogative," she said firmly.

Perhaps she was right. The trouble was that he had never grown used to thinking of himself as an employer.

3

After leaving Richard Monk's office, Berg walked to Holborn and into the nearest coffee bar. Because he hadn't been able to eat any breakfast, he bought a Danish pastry to eat with his coffee. But this proved to be a mistake as it was stale and tasted of sawdust with a faint flavour of apricot syrup round the edges. He chose a table as far from the door as he could find and sat there sipping his coffee, having discarded the Danish pastry after two eroding nibbles.

He had telephoned his office on his way to Monk's and told his secretary not to expect him till later in the morning. He now had the rather enjoyable sensation of the professional truant and, to his surprise, felt no urge to get back to work. Far removed though it was from his normal routine, he was finding it not disagreeable to sit and think and not worry about time. The truth was that he was still numbed by recent events and was unsure whether it would all turn out to have been one of those non-dimensional dreams or whether his life had undergone a cathartic change from which it could never fully recover. All he knew at the moment was that his visit to Monk had brought him relief. Whatever lay ahead, he felt that he now had someone to whom he could turn. Someone who would be ready to hold his hand if things began to develop badly. And, curious suspended state though he felt himself in, he had no illusions that they might develop badly.

He carried his empty cup over to the counter and asked for another coffee.

"If you go and sit down, the waitress'll bring it to you." The matronly female who presided behind the hissing machine which brewed coffee somewhere in its intestines spoke in a coldly rebuking tone and Berg was made to feel that he'd been caught out trying to avoid tipping the waitress. However, he made no protest and returned silently to his place. When the coffee arrived, he gave the girl sixpence which she accepted with perfunctory thanks without glancing to see what it was.

"Finished with that?" she enquired, nodding at the Danish pastry.

"Yes, thanks."

"Something wrong with it?"

"It's stale."

"They go off quickly, those things," she remarked with casual interest. "Like something else instead?"

"No, thanks."

"Sure?"

"Absolutely. The coffee's sufficient."

She wandered away and left Berg once more with his thoughts.

Half an hour later he reluctantly put on his coat and left. He could easily have passed the whole day there drinking successive cups of coffee. However, the sight of his office and, in particular, of the pile of letters and invoices and order forms awaiting his attention did something to restore his sense of normality. Apart from anything else, there was the need to continue earning a living—at least until the police put a full stop to it.

His secretary, Miss Steen, came in as soon as she heard him in the room.

"Hello, Beth," he said, "sorry I'm so late. I got held up."

She looked at him with a worried expression.

"Held up? I thought you said on the telephone that something had happened over the weekend?"

"Yes, that's what I meant."

"Are you . . . are you feeling quite all right?"

"Yes, I'm all right," he said, while he vaguely picked up papers off his desk and, after an abstracted glance, put them down again.

"There's nothing urgent amongst that lot. It can all wait or Mr. Femmer can deal with most of it, if you're *not* all right."

He sighed. "I've had a bit of a shock, Beth. It sounds absolutely crazy put like this, but I may be charged with murder."

"Not Hilda?" she blurted out.

It was Berg's turn to look startled. "Hilda? Oh, no, this is something quite different. It's nothing to do with Hilda. She doesn't know anything about it at all. It's something I've not even been able to talk to you about, Beth. And I still can't tell you everything."

"What murder are you talking about then?"

"A man named Parsons."

"Parsons? Parsons?" she repeated, to his faint irritation. "Who do you know called Parsons?"

"He was a civil servant. I only knew him slightly."

"But why should *you* be charged with his murder?"

"It's a very long story, but it looks as if I've been made the victim of circumstances. Believe me, Beth, I didn't murder him."

"Of course you didn't. But if only you'd tell me more, I might be able to help."

"I can't tell you more, yet. You must just continue to trust me as you've trusted me for so long. Nobody knows as much even as I've told you except for the solicitor I've been to see this morning. Hilda knows nothing. You're the first friend I've been able to talk to."

Beth Steen shook her head disbelievingly. "I can't believe it! *You* suspected of murder!" She let out a mirthless laugh. "And to think I automatically assumed it was Hilda. That was a case of the wish being father to the thought."

"Don't talk like that, Beth. It's not Hilda's fault."

"Whose is it then?"

"In so far as it's anyone's, it's mine," he said quietly.

"Oh, Joe," she said with a slight catch in her voice. She moved towards him, but stopped suddenly when there was a knock on the door and it opened to reveal Patrick Femmer, who was the firm's office manager.

"I'm sorry, do I intrude?" he asked cheerfully. He glanced from Berg to Miss Steen with a fixed smile on his normally rather melancholy face.

"Mr. Berg is not feeling very well this morning," Miss Steen said quickly.

"Oh, I'm sorry to hear that. I'd heard you weren't coming in till late. Perhaps it would have been better to have stayed at home today."

"I shall be all right, thanks, Patrick, though I'd be grateful if you'd deal with as much of this stuff as you can."

"Of course. Let me take it now. I'll keep any queries until you're feeling better." He picked up the pile of correspondence and was about to go when Berg spoke again.

"It's possible I may have to go away for a few days at short notice. If that does happen, I'd like you to run the business in my absence. I know it'll be in safe hands with you and Miss Steen."

Femmer's expression showed concern as he said, "I'm sure Miss Steen and I will do our best to hold the fort if you do have to go away."

After he had gone out of the room, Berg said, "It was a bright day when he joined the firm. He's picked up the work amazingly quickly. Makes me wonder how I put up with that useless fellow Werter for as long as I did."

"Femmer's certainly much more efficient," Miss Steen agreed. "Let's hope he won't be lured away by a competitor. That's always the danger. The really good managers in this business are as few and far between as icicles on the Equator."

Something in her tone made Berg ask, "You get on all right with him, don't you?"

"With Patrick Femmer? Certainly."

"But not too well, I trust," he added in an attempt at jocularity.

Beth Steen's reply was to give him an infinitely sad smile and kiss him quickly on the brow.

"Has it ever occurred to you, Joe, that the only reason Hilda has never suspected anything is because I'm almost as old as she is and manage to look so much the staid secretary?"

"You flatter Hilda's interest in me," he said in a matter-of-fact tone, and then wished he hadn't. It was better that Beth should enjoy her illusions. That way meant fewer complications in their relationship.

4

Unless it was raining hard Richard usually made the journey on foot between his office and his flat, which was in a street just west of Berkeley Square. He enjoyed walking, even in London, and regarded the three or four miles he covered each day as doing more than anything else to keep him fit. This, coupled with no smoking and a natural dislike of spirits, enabled him to play five hard games of squash and appear no more done in at the end than a racehorse after a training canter over the downs.

Alan Scarby and he usually managed to play twice a week, and their matches had a now familiar pattern. Greater skill would give Alan the first two games, greater staying power would ensure that Richard won the last two. The middle game might go either way, though, of late, skill had been forced to bow to endurance at an increasingly early stage of their sweaty contests.

"It can't do me any good to feel as ill as this," Alan had jerked out between heavy pants after the last occasion.

"But think of the sense of well-being you'll have when you've showered and had a couple of pints," Richard had replied, bouncing up and down on the balls of his feet.

"One day I shan't get as far as any sense of well-being. I'll collapse on court and not all the coramine injections in the world will bring me round, and you'll have to tell Jane that I died chasing one of your sneaky shots."

"I can't think why you're not fitter," Richard replied in a genuinely puzzled tone. "It's not as though you're fat."

"Just because the Almighty saw fit to give you a second pair of lungs, reinforced steel calves and a dislike of smoking and gin, there's no need to sound so smug. I'm fitter than most married barristers of thirty-one. Come on, let's go and change and get to that sense of well-being."

Alan had telephoned Richard in the course of Monday afternoon and had agreed to call by his flat on his way home that evening. It was nearly seven o'clock when he arrived and Richard had been back nearly an hour. He had had a bath and was dressed in cream slacks and a black roll-neck sweater so that Alan, who was still in legal subfusc garb, said enviously: "You look just like an oasis to a desert traveller."

"Well, come in, desert traveller, and be refreshed."

Richard's flat could hardly have presented a more striking contrast with his office, the flat being furnished in modern Scandinavian style with the oddest shaped items serving various functional purposes. When friends asked, as they quite often did, whether he didn't fear he might get tired of it, he merely shrugged and said that it was possible, and that when he did he'd change it.

"What on earth is that, Richard?" Alan asked as they entered the living-room.

"A chair."

"Looks like a cross between a sawn-off Scotch egg and something from Jodrell Bank."

"It's a Finnish design. It revolves."

Alan shook his head in disbelief. "I've never seen anything quite like it."

"You're not supposed to have. It's brand new. Sit in it. Go on, don't be afraid, it's really very comfortable."

"Just like going back into the womb," Alan murmured as he backed himself into the chair. "It's comfortable all right," he said approvingly.

Richard handed him a glass. "One vodka and tonic."

"What's that you're drinking?"

"Moselle."

After a brief exchange of gossip, Alan said, "I mustn't stay too long, Richard, as I've promised Jane I'll be home by eight, so can we get on to the agenda's main item?"

Richard proceeded to tell him of Berg's visit. When he had finished, Alan said, "I read about the murder. After all, it's only about a mile from where we live. I know the Duchess of Bedford though I've never been inside. And you think he's told you the truth about his part in this?"

"I believe he has, though I wouldn't go so far as to say it's the whole truth. But I have a feeling that it's most of it."

"I agree that all you can do now is wait and see whether he's charged."

"If he is, I'd like you to take the brief, Alan."

Alan Scarby gave a cheerful smile. "I'll be delighted, of course, Richard. It has all the makings of an interesting case."

"But it doesn't half add to the burden when you really do believe that your client is innocent!"

"True. I wonder if my view of him will be the same as yours."

"Or whether mine will be the same after I've seen him again."

Alan nodded. "Are you proposing to get in touch with the police yourself?"

"No. I don't think it's a case for taking that initiative. I'd sooner wait in the wings until they move. I've told him not to say anything more without my being present."

"He's certainly said enough! If he's charged, he'll have only himself to blame. Lying to the police is always a singularly futile thing to do. Most people's lies have such short legs that they never get far before being caught and there's nothing the police relish more than a lying suspect. They become just like terriers who've been running in circles over a dozen different scents and suddenly fall upon a large plump rat. It's irresistible."

He drained his glass and thrust himself out of Richard's new chair.

"I must be on my way. Incidentally, I'm afraid I can't manage squash on Wednesday as I shall be at Maidstone Quarter Sessions all day. Can we make it Thursday instead?"

"That's all right for me. Why don't you get Jane to join us here for dinner afterwards? Tell her I've learnt some new recipes."

"That sounds fine provided we can lay on the baby-sitter."

"How is my god-daughter?"

"Adorable."

"If you can't get the baby-sitter, bring her too. She can sleep in my bedroom."

"She's a bit old for carting about at nights. Anyway, some of this furniture might give her nightmares."

The telephone suddenly rang and Richard walked across to answer it, while Alan hovered at the door.

"Hello . . . yes, speaking . . . Oh, good evening, Mr. Berg . . . half-past eight? . . . no, that's all right. I'll be there."

Alan looked at him enquiringly as he replaced the receiver.

"Developments?"

"Detective-Inspector Pullar has just 'phoned him and will shortly be on his way out to Hendon to see him."

"I thought you said the officer's name was Evans."

"I did. This man's Special Branch."

It took Monk three minutes to climb back into his suit and a further three to get round to the garage where he kept his car, a white Mercedes 230 SL coupé.

Despite losing his way a couple of times in Hendon, he still arrived at his destination with ten minutes to spare. Berg himself opened the front door, peering with an air of apprehension round it to see who his visitor was.

"Oh, it's you, Mr. Monk. Do come in. He hasn't arrived yet. I can't tell you how grateful I am to you for coming." He led the way into the front living-room and hurried across to switch off the television. "Fortunately, this is one of my wife's bridge evenings, so she doesn't know about this visitation. Do let me get you a drink. What'll you have?" He hovered in front of Richard who had sat down on the sofa.

Richard shook his head. "Nothing now, thanks. Did Inspector Pullar say exactly what he wanted?"

"No. He just said there was something urgent he wished to see me about and could he come round this evening. I tried to find out what it was, but he said he preferred not to discuss it on the 'phone. Though he was perfectly polite, he sounded a firm sort of individual."

"Apart from that, nothing further has happened since I saw you this morning? Inspector Evans hasn't been in touch with you again?"

"No. I suppose he and Inspector Pullar are working together on the case."

"I imagine Pullar's interested only in the Special Branch angle."

"That must mean that they know Parsons was engaged in . . . in . . . in giving away information."

Richard had the impression that Berg had been about to say "espionage", but had shied away from using this chilling word in view of his own involvement.

"If they don't *know*, they must certainly *suspect*," he said.

There was the sound of a car drawing up outside and Berg sped across the room to peek round the end of the drawn curtain.

"I think it's them," he said nervously. "There are two of them."

"They usually hunt in pairs," Richard remarked.

A few seconds later the doorbell rang and Berg left the room to admit his visitors. From a rear view he might have been someone mounting the scaffold rather than passing into the hall of his own home.

Richard heard a polite murmur of voices and then a tall, rather distinguished-looking man with iron-grey hair and an expression which matched came into the room. He paused on catching sight of Richard and glanced enquiringly at Berg.

"This is Mr. Monk, my solicitor," Berg said with a nervous catch in his voice.

Detective-Inspector Pullar's urbanity seemed to desert him for a moment.

"You didn't tell me you were going to ask your solicitor to come," he said crossly. Turning to Richard he added, "I had hoped to be able to speak to Mr. Berg in confidence on a matter of some delicacy."

"You're not disputing my right to be present?"

"Not the right, only the necessity."

"That's a matter for Mr. Berg."

"I asked Mr. Monk to come and I'd like him to stay," Berg said emphatically.

Inspector Pullar pursed his lips in disapproval. "Very well, then. May I sit down?"

He did so without waiting for an answer, and the fresh-faced young man with him followed suit on an upright chair, pulling out a shorthand notebook from his jacket pocket and carefully unscrewing the cap of an ancient fountain pen.

"This is Detective-Constable Dixon who will be taking a note of things," Inspector Pullar said in an off-hand manner. He leaned forward, resting his arms on those of the chair and lacing his fingers. He stared at Berg in silent appraisal for a full half minute before speaking. "How long had you known Mr. Parsons?"

"Between four and five years."

"How did you first come to know him?"

"We met socially."

"And would it be right to say that you got to know him well over the years?"

"No, it wouldn't."

"Not?" Inspector Pullar queried in well-bred surprise.

"No, I didn't know him very well at all."

"You knew what his job was?"

"Only that he was a civil servant in the Ministry of Defence."

"Did he ever talk about his work there?"

"Not to me."

"But you knew the rough nature of his duties?"

"No, I didn't at all."

"Not at all?" Once more Inspector Pullar's tone held a note of politely disbelieving surprise.

"All I knew was that he worked in some technical branch of the Ministry."

"Ah! So you did at least know that. Are you sure he never described his work to you? Never told you what form of research his branch was responsible for?"

"I didn't know he was concerned in any research."

"I'm using the word in its widest sense. I don't mean he was one of these white-overalled workers bent over a microscope."

"All I knew was that he was employed in the Ministry of Defence."

"And in a technical capacity? You've just said you knew that!"

"Yes," Berg agreed wearily.

"Did you ever meet any of his colleagues?"

"No."

Inspector Pullar picked a piece of cotton off his trousers and dropped it fastidiously over the side of the chair.

"Did you ever hear him express any political views?"

"No, never."

"Never?" Again the note of polite disbelief. "Do you mean that even after five years you had no idea which way he was politically inclined?"

"I never heard him discuss politics. Anyway, I though civil servants were supposed not to declare any political allegiance."

"The same applies to police officers, of course, but I don't imagine there's anyone who has known me for five years who doesn't know where my political sympathies lie."

Richard felt he had a very reasonable notion after five minutes.

Berg gave a helpless shrug. "I can only repeat that I've no idea how Mr. Parsons voted."

"Did he have any foreign friends?"

"I didn't meet any."

"Did he ever mention any foreign contacts?"

Berg looked anxiously across at Richard who said, "Isn't it time, Inspector, that you told Mr. Berg why you are asking him all these questions?"

Inspector Pullar turned his head as though to see where this unwanted interruption had come from. In a tone of lofty reproof he said, "When a civil servant, who in the course of his work has had daily access to classified material, is suddenly found murdered in highly peculiar circumstances, the public interest requires a great number of questions to be asked."

"I'm not disputing that," Richard replied tartly, "but if you want Mr. Berg's full co-operation in answering your questions, I should have thought it in your own interest to tell him why you're asking them. It's entirely up to you, of course, but unless you can produce a satisfactory answer, I might feel obliged to give Mr. Berg certain advice."

Inspector Pullar flashed him a look of undiluted dislike. Turning back to Berg he said icily, "I'm investigating the possibility—and I put it no higher than that—that Mr. Parsons may have been enagaged in activities which make his death of interest to the security authorities. I can't say more than that, but I hope it is sufficient to satisfy your solicitor of the necessity for my questions." He leaned further forward and assumed an expression of grave self-importance. "My question was whether Mr. Parsons ever mentioned any foreign contacts to you?"

Berg again gave Richard a look of anxious enquiry.

"I think you told me," Richard remarked, "that he once mentioned to you a man by the name of Gamel."

"That's right," Berg said in a relieved voice.

"Gamel has a foreign sound about it."

"What do you know about Gamel?" Inspector Pullar asked sharply, ignoring Richard.

"Only that Mr. Parsons said he was somebody he'd met once or twice."

"Go on, tell me more," Inspector Pullar said with quiet insistence.

"There isn't any more to tell. I've never met Gamel, I don't know anything about him. I only know that he was an acquaintance of Mr. Parsons'."

"If you know that much, you must know more. How did the dead man ever come to mention his name to you in the first place?"

Berg bit worriedly at a loose piece of skin on his lower lip. "It was when we were walking home one evening from the Underground, he just happened to say he had to go out again to meet this man called Gamel."

Inspector Pullar frowned with displeasure. "Look, Mr. Berg, if when I leave here tonight, I happen to mention I'm going to see Mr. Manescu, it would sound pretty odd, wouldn't it? In fact it wouldn't make any sense, would it? You'd wonder what on earth I was talking about, wouldn't you? Unless, of course, you knew who Manescu was and I'd already told you something of my association with him." He paused and then said grimly, "Have I made myself clear?"

"It won't help you to browbeat my client," Richard broke in. "He's already told you that he knows nothing about Gamel apart from his name."

"And I've already made it plain that I can't accept that as being the truth," Inspector Pullar said in a grating tone. "He must know more. If Parsons went as far as mentioning Gamel's name, he must have said more. All I want to know is how much more." He turned and gave Richard a hard stare. "This isn't a matter of mere personal relationships. The national interest could be involved. I think you ought to understand that, Mr. Monk, and perhaps you'll feel less inclined to treat this interview as a session of the school debating society."

Richard flushed angrily. "You might try behaving less like a deus ex machina and see what happens. If you can." He shook his head as though to dispel his burst of temper. "It's not going to help if we get cross with each other, so let me see if I can answer your question. As he has already told you, Mr. Berg has never met Gamel. He knows of him only through Mr. Parsons, and Mr. Parsons not long ago did mention to Mr. Berg that he was afraid of Gamel."

"Why should he have told Mr. Berg that?" Inspector Pullar asked silkily.

"I suppose because he had already mentioned him as an acquaintance to Mr. Berg."

"That's not very convincing."

"It's speculation and no more."

The Special Branch man switched his attention back to Berg. "Do you have business interests in the Middle East?"

"With Israel, yes."

"With Egypt?"

"No."

"Jordan, Syria, Iraq, Lebanon?"

"No."

Inspector Pullar frowned. "Only with Israel?"

Berg nodded. "I'm on the Arabs' black-list."

"Oh." He sounded nonplussed.

It seemed to Monk that Inspector Pullar had been working on the assumption that Parsons, Berg and Gamel had together been in the same boat and all pulling in the same direction. He obviously knew about Gamel and had been hoping to find evidence of ties between him and Parsons and Berg. These hopes had now been dashed since they were founded on a false premise. What he, Richard, had to decide and decide quickly, was how much more it would be in his client's interest to say at this stage. The danger of saying too much was that it would reveal Berg's part in the affair in its somewhat ambiguous light. But to say too little was to fail to point out the right direction for the police to carry their enquiries. He thought hard for a minute or two and finally decided that so long as his client remained at large the less he said, the better. Should he be arrested for Parsons' murder, then would be the moment to put the police fully on to Gamel's track. However, this didn't mean he couldn't try and probe a little further himself.

"You obviously know more about this man Gamel than my client does," he said. "Would it be indiscreet to enquire whether you have yet interviewed him?"

Inspector Pullar stuck out his lower lip and touched it thoughtfully with a finger.

"I don't know why I should answer that, but as a matter of fact we haven't. Mr. Gamel is not an easy person to keep track of and we've temporarily lost touch with him. I was hoping you might be able to help us find him, Mr. Berg," he added in meaningful tone. He rose to his feet. "Our little chat has not been as productive as I had hoped, but I'm not a person who is easily put off and we shall doubtless have another in due course." He moved toward the door. "By the way, may I have a look at your passport while I'm here?"

"It's upstairs, I'll fetch it," Berg said and disappeared from the room.

"That your Mercedes outside, Mr. Monk?" Inspector Pullar asked idly, while they waited for him.

"Yes."

"Very handsome car. Is your office out this way?"

"No, Bedford Square."

"Bedford Square?" Inspector Pullar echoed vaguely. "Haven't I read something about you?"

"You may have."

"Yes, I remember now. Wasn't it you who defended that chap in C.I. who was framed?"

"Detective-Sergeant Jimson, you mean? Yes, I represented him."

"Of course, now I know who you are." He stared at Richard in thoughtful appraisal. "Well, well. . . that's interesting. Most interesting. Some people at the Yard seem to regard you as quite a Sir Galahad."

"That's fanciful."

"Those sort of labels usually are. In the same way that one country's traitors are another's heroes."

Their eyes met in an impassive exchange.

"Here's my passport," Berg said, returning to the room.

Inspector Pullar examined each page in turn before handing it back. "Thank you, Mr. Berg," he said without any indication of whether it confirmed or disproved what he was expecting.

"Good night, Mr. Monk."

"Good night, Inspector."

Detective-Constable Dixon nodded a farewell as he followed his chief out of the room. It only then occurred to Richard that he had not uttered a single word throughout the evening. A portable tape-recorder would have been just as useful to Inspector Pullar, and probably more accurate.

Berg returned to the room from seeing the visitors off and went straight over to a walnut cocktail cabinet.

"Surely you'll have a drink now, Mr. Monk? Whisky? Gin?"

"I'll have a bitter lemon if you have one."

Berg handed him the drink, fetched himself a brandy and soda and sat down opposite, after lighting a cigarette. Richard noticed that his hands trembled slightly.

"How did you think it went?" he asked. "I didn't put my foot in it?"

"I doubt whether you said anything to allay Inspector Pullar's suspicions that you could tell him more if you wanted, but I think that was unavoidable. This was not the moment to reveal your own certainty that it was Gamel who murdered Parsons. You couldn't do that without inviting a whole string of further pertinent questions, and it was better to keep quiet."

"Do you still think I'm a suspect?"

"I'm afraid you must be. That's why we had to tread carefully with Pullar, since he'd have certainly passed on to Inspector Evans anything of interest to him from the murder angle."

Berg took a noisy gulp of his drink. "It's awful to be kept in suspense like this. How long do you think it'll go on?"

"I can't tell you. I'm afraid it's something you have to learn to adjust to." He swilled the remains of his drink round the bottom of the glass while staring into it as if it were a crystal ball. Suddenly looking up, he asked, "Have you been in touch with Mrs. Parsons since her husband's death?"

"I dropped her a note of sympathy yesterday. But that's all."

"How well do you know her?"

"Not at all well. Why?"

"I was wondering whether we could go round and see her."

"Now?"

"Yes, now. How far away does she live?"

"Ten minutes' walk."

"Let's 'phone and see if she's there. Do you know the number? I'll speak to her."

Richard was beginning to think no one was going to answer when he heard the receiver lifted and a woman's voice came on the line.

"Is that Mrs. Parsons?" he asked.

"Yes."

"My name is Richard Monk. I'm Mr. Berg's solicitor and with him at the moment. I'd be very grateful if Mr. Berg and I could come round and see you for a few minutes."

"I don't really feel like seeing anyone now."

"I promise you it won't take long and it is rather important."

"Very well," she said, doubtfully, "but my nerves are not very good."

"I can quite understand that, Mrs. Parsons, and I'll do my best to see that our visit doesn't upset you. We'll be round in a few minutes."

They were on the point of leaving when the telephone rang and Berg dashed back into the living-room. Richard heard him say: "Oh, it's you, Beth. . . . I'm afraid I can't stop now, I'll try and call you later. It'll depend on what time Hilda gets back. . . . No, I'm about to go out. Mr. Monk's here. . . ."

He made no reference to his caller when he rejoined Richard, who was left wondering.

Mrs. Parsons was a short, flat-chested, honey-coloured woman whose face was dominated by a pair of pale blue framed spectacles, which looked as if they'd been invented for someone with a face twice the dimensions of hers. She led the way into a room in which another honey-coloured woman was sitting knitting.

"This is my sister, Mrs. Pepper, who is staying with me."

Mrs. Pepper rolled up her knitting and thrust it into a capacious bag on the floor beside her. "I think I'll go up to my room now, Doris," she said and departed after acknowledging her sister's visitors with a markedly suspicious glance.

37

"It's possible," Richard said pleasantly, "that you're not without knowledge of the reason for our visit." The wary look she threw Berg confirmed this. He went on, "I expect the police have been asking you a good many questions these last three days and they may also have imparted to you some of their information."

"I don't really know whether I ought to be talking to you," Mrs. Parsons said with another uneasy look in Berg's direction. "The inspector told me to be careful what I said to . . . to anyone who came round to see me."

"Look, Mrs. Parsons, it'll be best if I'm absolutely frank with you. Mr. Berg knows that the police suspect him of having been involved in your husband's unhappy death. He knows even better that he's completely innocent in the matter. He wouldn't be able to come and sit in your drawing-room if it were otherwise."

"I can't think who could want to kill Fred," she said tearfully.

"Certainly Mr. Berg didn't, though I take it the police asked you about him."

She nodded. "They wanted to know how long Fred had known him and . . . and how often they used to meet."

"What did you tell them, Mrs. Parsons?"

"I just told them the truth."

"Which was . . .?"

"That Fred had known Mr. Berg about four or five years, and that I didn't know how often they used to meet."

"Did your husband have a younger brother?"

"Malcolm, do you mean? He was killed at the time of Suez."

"Was your husband very fond of him?"

"Yes, he was almost like a father to him. He was sixteen years older than Malcolm. But why are you asking me about that?"

"Didn't the police?"

"No."

"Did the police tell you, Mrs. Parsons, why they thought your husband had been murdered?"

"No. They just asked a lot of questions about his work and whether he used to discuss it with me."

"Did they say why they suspected Mr. Berg?"

"Because my husband had an appointment with him last Friday evening. It was in his diary."

"Had your husband told you where he was going that evening?"

Her lower lip began to tremble and she pressed a thumbnail against it. "He'd told me he'd be working late that night."

"Did he often stay late in the office?"

"Not very often," she said, trying to blink away her tears before they could run down her cheek.

"Did you ever hear your husband mention the name of Gamel?"

She shook her head. "They asked me that, too." She looked accusingly at Berg, who was sitting over in the corner with an air of silent anguish. "What do you know about Fred's death?" she asked with surprising vehemence. "Why was he going to meet you that night?"

"I promise you, Mrs. Parsons, I didn't kill him," Berg said miserably.

"But you know who did?" she demanded in an outburst of emotion.

"Mrs. Parsons, you've been extremely kind and helpful," Richard broke in quickly, "and I don't want our visit to be the cause of further distress to you."

"If you want to know," she said dully, " the police believe that Fred was passing Ministry information to someone. They think that was why he was killed. They didn't actually say so but I could tell that was what they thought." She looked across at Berg again. "And you were in it, too, weren't you? Why otherwise should they suspect you?"

"I did not kill your husband, Mrs. Parsons. I swear it on the Holy Book."

"How do I know whether to believe you or not," she asked helplessly, "when you were having meetings with Fred which I knew nothing about? Why were you having these secret meetings?"

"I wasn't . . ." he began.

"Did your wife know you were meeting my husband?"

"I think it would be better if we left," Richard said rising to his feet. "I can well understand your feelings, Mrs. Parsons."

"Can you! What's going to happen to me now! Two boys still at school, no money and their father's name smeared across the newspapers."

It seemed to Richard that her hysteria was mounting all the

while they remained, so he darted from the room in search of the sister. A light shone beneath the door of an upstairs room and he knocked on it.

"We're just going, Mrs. Pepper. I'm afraid your sister is rather upset. Perhaps you could come down."

The door opened and Mrs. Pepper pushed past him without a word. They let themselves out of the house with a furtiveness of which each was uncomfortably aware.

"Our visit did at least serve one purpose," Berg said quietly as they regained the car. "She provided confirmation of what I've told you about Parsons. I wasn't sure before whether you believed me, but now I know you must."

Richard forebore to point out that the visit had also served to emphasise the aura of suspicion which surrounded his client.

When they arrived back at his house, Berg said, "I hope you won't mind if I don't ask you in, but I see that my wife is back."

Richard made an appropriate murmur. Should her husband be arrested and charged with murder he wondered whether Mrs. Berg would be as shocked as the victim's wife had appeared to be at her husband's death. According to Sheila, either their marriages were at fault or they must have known something.

He drove straight home and went to bed.

5

The next day Richard had enough to occupy him without giving Berg more than an occasional thought. It seemed safe to assume that no news was good news in the sense that the police still hadn't found enough evidence to justify charging his client. But it was rather nerve-racking wondering exactly what they were up to and how successful their burrowing was. All he knew from experience was that it was never safe to tell a client in these sorts of circumstances that the steam was off and that he could relax. In this connection police enquiries enjoyed the same properties attributed to the mills of God, which was encouraging for everyone save those caught up in the machinery.

That evening he was invited to dinner with Sheila and her husband. She had tendered the invitation with a good deal of diffidence and been apparently gratified by his willing acceptance. Richard thought she probably wanted him to see what a clever husband she had, her husband to take stock of his wife's employer, and each of them to realise how fortunate he was in having such a secretary and such a wife.

He enjoyed himself on the whole, though there were moments when he wondered how Sheila had come to marry a neurotic bore. Then he noticed the protective gleam in her eye and knew the answer. Also it wasn't fair to write Harold Gillam off as a neurotic bore. He was certainly neurotic, but he only became a bore in the final stages of the evening when he had had rather too much to drink and held fourth on the unsung nuances of Ingmar Bergman's latest film which, as far as Richard gathered, he had seen five afternoons running and was proposing to see on the next five.

It was half past ten when Richard left the Gillams to drive home. His telephone was ringing as he opened his front door and managed to convey that it had been doing so all the time he had been out.

Against a background of muffled sounds a voice enquired, "Is that Mr. Monk?" followed by, "Hold on a moment, sir, someone wants to speak to you."

"Mr. Monk, it's Joseph Berg. I'm at the police station. They've arrested me. Can you come at once?"

"Which station?"

"Fulham."

"Have you been charged?"

"No. I insisted that you should be here and they said they'd wait till you were."

Richard never ceased to be struck by the insistence of his clients that he should be at their side during what was an entirely formal process.

"I'll come along at once," he said dutifully. "How long have you been there?"

"About an hour and a half."

"You haven't made a statement or anything like that?"

"No."

"Good. I'll be with you in about twenty minutes."

When he arrived at the police station, he was taken to a room in which two men could just be discerned through the cloud of stale cigarette smoke which hung like the aftermath of a grenade explosion.

"Mr. Monk? I'm Detective-Superintendent Kettleman. This is Detective-Inspector Evans. Can I offer you anything? Tea? Coffee? I can't really recommend either, but the inspector and I are addicts after all these years." He ruefully surveyed the cups and saucers which were strewn over the desk and on top of two filing cabinets.

Superintendent Kettleman was a large, amiable-looking man with fair hair and the beginnings of a paunch. Inspector Evans, as befitted one whose origins lay in a Welsh mining valley was shorter and had sharp features and thick black hair of a wiry texture.

"No, I don't want anything, thanks. I've recently had a good dinner."

"So you're representing our friend Berg," Kettleman said in a ruminative tone. "He seems quite a decent sort of bloke."

Richard said nothing. It usually meant that the police thought they had a strong case when they took time off to tell you they liked your client.

"Well, I expect you'd like to have a word with him before he's charged," Kettleman went on. He picked up the cup at his elbow, drained it and made a face. "There's only one thing nastier than station tea and that's cold station tea. Come on, I'll take you down."

Berg was sitting dejectedly on a bench in a small room at the back of the general office. A constable sat facing him, as though waiting for an egg to hatch.

"That's all right, Fields, you can wait outside," Kettleman said to him. "Let me know when you've finished, Mr. Monk. And maybe afterwards you'd like to have another word with me."

Some of the stale atmosphere of the police station seemed to have rubbed off on to Berg. He looked tired and rumpled.

"You'd better tell me everything from the beginning," Richard said briskly.

"They came about a quarter to nine. There were three of them, the Superintendent, Inspector Evans and another one. They said they were going to arrest me and bring me here where

I'd be charged with Parsons' murder. I tried to 'phone you, but I couldn't get any answer and they said it'd be time enough if you came along to the station later."

"And you haven't made any statements oral or written?"

"No. They said I could if I wished."

"I bet they did."

' "Oh, I forgot to mention that they searched the house before we left."

"Did they find anything?"

"There was nothing to find. They were mostly interested in papers and documents."

"Obviously trying to find further links between you and the dead man."

Berg shook his head in bewilderment. "How can I be charged when I'm innocent!"

"Now is the time when you have to be both patient and brave. It may be two or three weeks before we know the strength of the prosecution's case, and there's very little we can do in the meantime, other than go ahead quietly with preparations for your defence."

But Berg didn't appear to have been listening for he went on, "They've got to find Gamel. You've got to tell them now, Mr. Monk, that it was Gamel who murdered Parsons. Only Gamel can save me."

"You needn't worry about that. I have Gamel well in mind."

"But what'll happen if they can't find him?"

"There's every chance he will be found," Richard said with greater confidence than he felt. "Tell me, was your wife at home when the police came?"

"No, she was out at bridge again. They said they would let her know, but will you also get in touch with her?"

Richard nodded, though he felt no relish for the task.

"I was glad she wasn't there," Berg said. "Will you also please 'phone my office in the morning and tell my secretary, Miss Steen, what has happened?"

"Yes, I'll do that. Is there anyone to run things while you're in custody?"

"Patrick Femmer, my office manager, knows the ropes. He'll carry on."

"Right. Now just before we get on with the charging, I'd

better tell you what the next few steps are going to be. After you've been charged you'll spend the night here. Then tomorrow morning you'll appear in court—I'll be there—and the police will ask for a seven-day remand in custody. The magistrate's certain to grant that and you'll be taken to Brixton Prison. And I'll come and see you there, too. You'll also be able to have visitors there, so it won't be as bad as you probably imagine. Also you can go on wearing your own clothes as a prisoner on remand. I think that's about all for the moment. Anything you want to ask me before I tell them we're ready?"

Berg shook his head numbly. "I can't think of anything else."

"Well, don't worry, because I shall be seeing you in the morning, anyway. Unless you have contrary views, I propose to brief a counsel named Alan Scarby to defend you and I think it'll be best if we have him along at the lower court. Not tomorrow, since that'll be only a formality, but at future hearings."

"If you recommend him, Mr. Monk, that's good enough. Is he . . . forgive my asking this . . . but is he very expensive?"

"No, he won't break your bank. But we'll have a talk about the money side of your defence later on."

As Richard had learnt, part of the game in criminal work was knowing how far you could extend credit to what might be called the casual customers, those who walked in off the street and asked you to defend them, as Berg had done. The answer in a good many cases was not at all, but he didn't feel this was so with Berg. He just didn't seem like a debt defaulter, whatever else he might be.

Richard went to the door and indicated that he had finished speaking to his client. Shortly afterwards a small procession entered, consisting of Kettleman, Evans and an inspector in uniform holding out the charge sheet as though it were a sheet of music and he was about to burst into song. When he had said his piece, Berg, primed by Richard, replied, "I did not kill Frederick Parsons."

Richard bade his client good night and accompanied the two C.I.D. men upstairs.

"I'm aware of behaving just like a hospital nurse on these occasions," he said with a wry smile. "One tries to be sympathetic without being sentimental and brisk without being brusque."

"I should have thought the worst trap you can fall into in your job is to identify yourself with your client," Kettleman said.

"One certainly needs to remain objective. Of course, it's easier to do this in some cases than others. There are some clients with whom one has no inclination to identify oneself." He stifled a yawn. "But this is not the hour to launch into the philosophical niceties of a solicitor-client relationship. I'd much rather you told me the strength of the case you have got against Berg."

Kettleman laughed. "I know the prosecution don't have many secrets left these days, but we've not yet reached the stage when they're obliged to put all their wares in the police station window. It's not that I don't trust you, Mr. Monk; simply that our interests don't coincide in this particular deal."

"That means you're out to press the charge home if you can?"

"We wouldn't have preferred it if we didn't think the evidence was sufficient. It'll be up to a jury to say whether they agree."

"Can I ask if you've established a motive?" Kettleman pursed his lips and Richard added, "Let me tell you straightaway that what he said in answer to the charge is what he's said to me all along. It wasn't just one of those denials for the occasion."

Kettleman thoughtfully studied the burning tip of his cigarette. "We believe," he said carefully, "that your chap and the dead man were mixed up in some sort of spying racket. That's being dug into at the moment by the Special Branch people. But those are the present indications and, of course, life sells on the cheap side in those circles. Moreover," he added in a tough tone, "denials are what one expects from the pros in that business. They won't even admit, when caught, they had a mother and a father." He glanced toward Richard. "I don't know how that fits in with your information?"

"I'd certainly gathered there was a spy background, though, if what my client tells me is true, he was very much a fringe character and certainly never a murderer."

"If what he's told you is true," Kettleman observed sceptically.

"I'm not entirely empty-handed over this. You see, Berg doesn't just say, 'I didn't do it', he has instructed me to give you the name of the man who, he believes, did murder Parsons."

Kettleman, who had been fiddling with a paper-clip, looked up sharply. "And who is that?"

"Someone called Gamel."

"I've heard that name."

"Inspector Pullar mentioned it," Evans said.

"That's right, he did. Well, Mr. Monk, you'd better tell me a bit more about this Gamel chap, if you want me to do something about it."

When Richard had finished speaking, Kettleman said, "Not very much, is it? A name, no address, no nothing else. I thought you were going to offer me Mr. Gamel on a plate, not just point to the haystack and invite me to search for a needle which may or may not be in it."

"At least you know he exists."

"Do I?"

"Inspector Pullar confirms that."

"And why should I set off on what could be a wild goose chase on the unsupported word of your client?"

Richard bit his lip. He said: "Will you treat what I now tell you as being right off the record?"

"I thought the whole of this was off the record."

"Good enough. I can assure you, Superintendent, that Berg has the best of reasons for his statement that Gamel murdered Parsons."

"You mean he saw it happen?"

Richard met the superintendent's steady stare but said nothing.

"So that's it?" Kettleman murmured. "So that's what he's saying, is it? That he was there and saw it happen? It's a bit different from what he told Inspector Evans last Saturday. He told Inspector Evans that he had an appointment with a business friend at a public house in Mayfair. That was his story then."

"Since when you've doubtless been able to disprove it?" Richard said.

"Certainly, we can prove he lied," Kettleman replied energetically.

"And of course it's your case that he was in Starforth Street and not in a Mayfair pub," Richard's tone was sweetly reasonable.

"I daresay, but it's not my case that he saw somebody else murder Parsons."

"No, but it's his case that somebody else did. That Gamel

did. Which brings us back to the starting point." Richard stood up. "I'll put it in writing if it'll help, but the defence are formally asking you to search for Gamel. I know you're not obliged to, but I'm sure you would want to help the defence in the circumstances. After all, you have the resources and we don't. Moreover, you can be quite certain that Gamel's name will crop up throughout the trial, and the judge will doubtless wish to know what efforts have been made to find him."

Superintendent Kettleman gave Richard a stony look. "You've made your point clear enough, Mr. Monk, though I could have done without the veiled threats."

"I assure you . . ."

Kettleman waved aside his protest and went on, "However, each of us now has some idea where the other stands and that's no bad thing. At the moment, Special Branch are looking for Gamel, because they're more interested in him than we are here. Though if and when he is found, I don't doubt I shall have a few questions to put to him myself."

Richard realised that he had nettled the superintendent, though this had certainly not been his intention. He had simply wished to make it plain beyond anyone's doubt that the defence were not merely denying that Berg had committed the murder but were positively asserting that Gamel had. Unfortunately, Kettleman had chosen to take this as a personal slap in the face and had removed himself on to a lofty pedestal. Because he had been agreeable and helpful to Richard, he seemed to resent the suggestion that public duty and even self-interest, rather than goodwill, should make him assist the defence further. Richard had come across the attitude before, one to which the police were especially prone. Their goodwill frequently knew no limits, but hint that goodwill alone might not be sufficient and they could become as prickly as holly leaves.

He was about to make a further attempt at propitiation when the telephone rang. Superintendent Kettleman listened in silence for a moment, then thrust the receiver at him. "You better take this call. It's your client's wife."

It was perhaps as well that he had no time to prepare himself for the call, since he had not looked forward with any relish to his first contact with Mrs. Berg. As it was, he had no time to dwell on his inhibited feelings.

"This is Richard Monk, Mrs. Berg. I'm the solicitor representing your husband. I was going to get in touch with you shortly."

"Mr. Monk, did you say?"

"Yes, M-O-N-K."

"Oh!" she sounded nonplussed.

"I'm sorry, I'm not clear where you come from, Mr. Monk. Are you with French and Pollock?"

"No, I'm Richard Monk of Richard Monk & Co. Your husband came and consulted me yesterday." He looked at his watch. "I know it's late, Mrs. Berg, but if you don't mind staying up, I think it might be best if I came out to see you tonight."

"I think perhaps it would. I just don't understand what's going on. What about Joe?"

"He'll be spending the night at the police station."

"Is it true that he's been charged with killing Mr. Parsons?"

"I'm afraid it is."

"I can't believe it's happening," she said in a bemused tone. "I feel I must be dreaming it."

"I'll be with you in just under half an hour and I'll try and explain everything then."

Richard found that he was sweating as he put the receiver back. He took out his handkerchief and passed it across his forehead, then squeezing it into a ball rubbed his palms.

Superintendent Kettleman gave him an amused smile. "I always enjoy seeing someone else work for their money. It's turning out to be quite a busy evening for you." He yawned cavernously and added, "Well, I'm going home and to bed. It'll be a nice change to think of *someone else* still out on the job as my head hits the pillow. See you at court in a few hours' time."

The house out at Hendon seemed familiar, but different. Richard was bothered until he realised that the difference was attributable to Mrs. Berg's own presence. The presence of someone he had never met before but who moved around completely at home in surroundings he associated with someone else, namely her husband.

She was a short, rather dumpy woman with jet black hair and a face which was square without being hard or masculine. She was heavily made-up and had calm brown eyes which gave her an air of watchful repose.

Richard sat down in the same chair he had occupied the previous evening.

"I'm afraid this must have come as a horrible shock to you," he said.

She made a fluttering motion with her hands to indicate that this was by way of being a massive understatement.

"Please tell me what it's all about. So far I've done nothing but answer questions without being told why they were being asked."

"Who's been asking you the questions?"

"An Inspector Pullar. He only left shortly before I 'phoned the police station."

"I'm afraid I also need to ask you some questions, Mrs. Berg, but first let me give you the bare facts of the case. Yesterday morning your husband came to see me at my office. He told me that he thought he might be suspected of the murder of Frederick Parsons. Unhappily, as we now know, his suspicions were well founded, although he also told me with great insistence that he was not guilty, and he gave me the name of the man who had killed Mr. Parsons. All that is now in the hands of the police. I did also gather from your husband that he hadn't told you anything about all this."

"I didn't know a thing," she replied in an affronted tone. "Joe never has discussed his business affairs with me, and I'm not the prying sort." She shook her head as though to clear it of its miasma of nightmare thoughts. "Is it really true that he's been involved in spying? That's what Inspector Pullar hinted; that Joe and Mr. Parsons were in some intrigue together. It's almost incredible! Why, we scarcely knew the Parsonses. We'd only met each other a few times at cocktail parties." She gave Richard a look in which resentment was mixed with enquiry.

"I have it from your husband's own lips that he and Mr. Parsons were engaged in something of the sort, though 'spying' is perhaps too strong a word to use in respect of your husband's part." When he had finished telling her the story, he said, "I gather from your expression that you knew absolutely nothing about this."

"I not only knew nothing, but I still find it almost impossible to believe."

"And you've never heard the name of Gamel before?"

"Never. The inspector asked me that as well in the course of a hundred other questions."

Richard looked at her with sympathy. He knew from vicarious experience the present chaos of her mind, her sensation of having been pole-axed without warning. More often than not it constituted one of the more bitter fruits of criminal conduct, the innocent wife stripped suddenly naked of the sense of security which she had long since come to accept as part of an immutable background to her life. He had seen it several times before, usually in fraud cases where a model husband of outward respectability and apparent wealth was shown to have been a swindler all the time. The great financial empire was seen to be worth no more than the paper on which the figures were written: the stout oak which supported it to be sawdust at the core. At the wave of a wand—or to be more exact at the execution of a warrant—smooth upper-crust comedy was turned into low kitchen-sink drama.

"This may sound a rather curious question, Mrs. Berg, but does it surprise you to learn that your husband lent himself to these activities?"

For several seconds she stared abstractedly at the wall behind his head.

"I know he's always felt for his people. He subscribes to several Jewish charities and has given his support to money-raising schemes for Jews, but he's never been a bigot. I sometimes used to think that he did it simply for conscience' sake, which I'm sure is a much more common motive than many would care to admit." She fell into a thoughtful silence for a few seconds. "No, I'm neither surprised nor am I not surprised, if you can follow that."

"You said *his* people just now. Do I take it from that that you are not a Jew?"

"My mother was Jewish, my father not. I have the blood in my veins, but I'm without most of the instincts. I'm certainly not a Zionist or anything of that nature."

"Have you met your husband's brother? The one who lives in Israel?"

"Years ago I met him. Now, he's a real zealot. Much more so than Joe."

Though she spoke of her husband with a certain fondness, Richard couldn't help feeling that it was the fondness evoked by turning the pages of the family album rather than some more immediate and vital reaction.

"I'm afraid this is going to be a long-drawn-out and worrying time for you, Mrs. Berg, and I'd like you to know that you can call upon my services any time you wish. It might be better if you went away for a while. It would save you being pestered by the Press. Have you anywhere you could go?"

She looked doubtful. "I think I'd prefer to stay here, unless things get too bad. How long will it all take?"

"At a guess the trial will come on in about a couple of months. Could be a bit less, could be a bit more."

"Shall I have to give evidence?"

"You can't be called to give evidence for the prosecution, and at the moment I can't see that there's very much evidence you could give on your husband's behalf. Evidence as to fact, that is. I'll be discussing all this with his counsel, but I doubt whether it helps him that his wife was ignorant of what was going on." Quickly he added, "I'm not suggesting it damns him either. It's just a negative which leaves the case where it is." He glanced at his watch. "It's one o'clock, Mrs. Berg, and if I'm going to be at court in the morning, it's time I made tracks for home."

"Ought I to come to court?"

Richard hesitated before replying. When he did so, his tone was strictly neutral. "There'll be no need for you to attend if you don't wish to. On the other hand, you'd probably be able to see your husband for a few minutes before he's taken to Brixton." He paused. "He might appreciate your being there."

"I expect there'll be someone there from the office," she said vaguely. "I'll see how I feel when I get up and decide then whether I can face the ordeal."

"So be it, Mrs. Berg. Incidentally, I shall need to interview various of your husband's employees."

"Perhaps they'll be able to help you more than I have," she said with a distant flicker of a smile. "Miss Steen has been his secretary for over five years. She may be able to tell you quite a lot."

As he drove back into central London it seemed to Richard that a whole lifetime had passed since he'd left the Gillam's earlier that evening. He had then intended going straight to bed and certainly nothing further was going to deter him from that object.

6

Every morning between ten and ten-thirty, only Sundays, Christmas Day and Good Friday excepted, in a score of depressing and unmistakably Victorian edifices of institutional appearance, a miscellaneous assemblage of people came together to present a scene of pure Hogarthian quality.

This was the hour when defendants and witnesses, together with their friends and relations and a rich handful of the capital's tribe of eccentrics, gathered in the ante-halls of London's Metropolitan Magistrates' Courts.

Defendants could be recognised by their generally strained looks. They stood in small knots with those who'd come to give them moral support, their eyes flicking anxiously at each new arrival. Their supporters tried to feed them morsels of comfort in small snatches of inappropriate conversation. It was usually a relief to both sides when the officer in charge of the case claimed his defendant and led him away to the jailer's office to await his appearance in court.

Witnesses stood about alone, longing for a kind word, but starting nervously when anyone did approach them. It was as if they expected threats and subornation from every quarter, and the evidence they had come to give had acquired the mystical purity of the Holy Grail.

The eccentrics were quite the most at home in this limbo and were there from a variety of motives. Not a few came simply in order to enjoy a morning of free warmth, others because their own twisted minds enabled them to appreciate the wriggling efforts of those haplessly impaled on a prong of the criminal law, others again to satisfy a ferocious interest in the law's minutiae, yet others out of an over-developed sense of audience participation. They spoke to no one and viewed each other with proper suspicion.

It was through such a throng that Richard pushed his way two minutes before half past ten. He glanced quickly round to see if Mrs. Berg had come. She wasn't there and he continued into court, just as Mr. Chaplin came on to the Bench to take his seat.

"Charlie", as he was known to all the court officials, was, in Richard's estimation, unique amongst the Metropolitan Magistrates, whose range of behaviour was known to run from charm to abrasive discourtesy and from expressions of detached patience to outbursts of childlike petulance.

Mr. Chaplin exhibited none of these traits. He sat silent and inscrutable and dispensed the nearest thing to computerised justice that had yet been invented. He was neither severe nor lenient, neither polite nor discourteous, and no one had yet discovered how far his patience extended since the business of his court was transacted with the quiet efficiency of pressurised salesmanship. He was the despair of newspapermen seeking headlines, but the joy of almost everyone else who came to his court.

Richard noticed that the large wall clock showed exactly half past ten as the magistrate nodded his readiness to start the day's work. He probably had "Made in Switzerland" stamped somewhere on his anatomy, Richard reflected.

For twenty minutes or so he watched a succession of defendants come and go, while Mr. Chaplin listened attentively to whoever stood up to address him. When silence fell and the human computer had been given all the available information about each defendant, it would, without any preliminary whirring noises, utter judgment. "Fined two pounds", "Three months' imprisonment", "Probation for twelve months" would come out in a dispassionate voice, and silence would fall again until the next case began.

A stir of interest at the Press table heralded Berg's appearance in the dock. He came quickly through the swing door, guided by the burly constable who served as jailer, and glanced round anxiously until he caught sight of Richard, who gave him a brief smile.

Detective-Superintendent Kettleman stepped into the witness-box.

"I respectfully ask for a remand in this case, your Worship."

Mr. Chaplin studied the slip of paper handed him by the usher and looked enquiringly across at Richard.

"I have no objections, sir."

The jailer came in on cue and said, "This day week, sir."

"You are remanded in custody until next Wednesday," Mr.

Chaplin said, speaking for the first and last time in the case that day.

Richard followed Berg through the swing door which led to the jailer's office.

"I'd like to have a word with him," he said to the assistant jailer.

"Certainly. Anything to oblige the defence," this officer replied heartily. "I take it Mr. Kettleman has no objections."

"I'm sure he hasn't. Anyway, here he is, you can ask him."

"'Morning, Mr. Monk," Kettleman said. "You look a bit black-ringed round the eyes. What were you up to last night?"

"Spare me the funnies," Richard said crisply. "I'd like to have a word with my client."

"Go ahead. I want to have a word with him myself later."

"Oh! What about?"

Kettleman laughed. "You needn't worry, I'm not going to beat a confession out of him."

"Then what?"

"The divisional surgeon will be along shortly and I want him to take a blood sample from your chap."

"Supposing he refuses?"

"I'm sure you wouldn't advise him to do that."

"Why not? You were going to do this without any reference to me."

"What rot, Mr. Monk, I'm asking you now if it'll be all right."

From his pleased expression Richard realised that he was merely being made the butt of Kettleman's playful revenge for the affront he'd given him the previous night in suggesting that the search for Gamel was a sacred duty.

All right, now let's call it quits, he thought, otherwise a game of tit-for-tat will turn into bloody warfare.

"Of course that's all right, Superintendent," he said with a poker face. "But try and leave him a pint in case you need some more later on."

Kettleman chuckled at the allusion. A good deal of publicity had been given to a recent case in which a young police officer had been carrying a carton containing blood and other human samples into court when the bottom fell out with results which made the court-room look like an operating theatre.

Berg looked up expectantly as his cell door was unlocked and

Richard entered. He had the tired expression of someone who can see no end to the black tunnel of misfortune in which he finds himself.

"The police want to take a blood sample from you. I've told them it would be all right."

"Why do they want a sample of my blood?" Berg asked anxiously.

"It's routine. They always want a control sample. They'll be testing all your clothing, which they took when you were arrested, for blood-stains, and if there are any, they'll want to determine whether it's yours or someone else's." He gazed down at his unhappy client. "I know you're feeling pretty low, but this is one of the worst parts. Once you get to Brixton you'll find that you adapt yourself to the regime of a remand prisoner. It's the unknown that's demoralising."

"It's the waiting and the uncertainty that I can't face."

"I know, but you've got to realise that the success of your defence will ultimately depend on yourself. Counsel and I can't make bricks without straw, and you're the only person who can supply the straw. And we want every piece you can lay hands on. I'll be coming to see you in a day or so, but in the meantime I want you to put down on paper every detail of the story you have told me from beginning to end. You may think you've already told me it all, but I bet you'll think of a dozen points you haven't yet mentioned. I want everything which touches on the case from the first moment you met Parsons to your arrest last night."

"All right, I'll do that."

Richard noticed his voice had lost some of its despair.

"I went to see your wife last night. As was to be expected, she was very upset and—"

"Was she in court this morning?" Berg broke in.

"I didn't see her. She wasn't sure whether she'd be coming or not."

"I'm glad she didn't. There's nothing she can do and I've let her down badly."

There was something in his tone which caused Richard to leave the subject, not that he had anything further to say on it. It was really no concern of his whether Mrs. Berg supported her husband or not. He was a criminal lawyer, not a marriage guidance counsellor, and the less he became involved in their domestic lives, the better for him.

"I shall want to interview members of your staff. I take it you have no objection?"

"All of them?"

"As many as have anything useful to say."

"I don't know what anyone of them can say," Berg remarked moodily.

"That'll be for me to find out," Richard replied with a smile. "I'd also like to get in touch with your brother in Israel."

Berg fidgeted and twice seemed to be on the point of saying something, but stopped. Richard remained silent and at length Berg said almost curtly, "I ought to warn you that you may find my secretary, Miss Steen, a rather emotional person. But Femmer, my office manager, is a sound chap. He'll be in charge while I'm away." His voice assumed a sudden note of self-pity. " 'While I'm away!' Supposing I'm never given the chance to go back! It's like going into hospital for a serious operation. One moment you talk about recovery, the next you think you'll never come out alive."

"It's not a bad analogy, provided you remember that the patient's will to live is often the decisive factor." He turned toward the door. "I must go now."

"You'll let me know if they find Gamel, won't you?" Berg asked eagerly.

"Certainly, I will. It may take a bit of time, but they'll get on to him in the end. It becomes less easy to vanish into thin air with every passing year."

Richard hoped he said it convincingly; he certainly didn't believe it.

As he emerged into the entrance hall of the court, a woman rose from one of the wall benches and came over to him.

"I was getting worried that I must have missed you. I thought you might have left by a different exit." She looked about her with distaste. "May I speak to you somewhere for a few minutes?"

"You've not yet told me who you are."

"No, of course. Because I knew you, I'd overlooked that you don't know me. I'm Elizabeth Steen, Mr. Berg's secretary."

"I was going to get in touch with you, Miss Steen. I take it you were in court just now?"

She nodded. "Is it possible to see him?"

Richard pursed his lips. "Come and have a cup of coffee, Miss

Steen," he said suddenly. "You can go and see Mr. Berg in Brixton Prison. It's more important for you to have a talk with me."

They were moving toward the main door when a man dashed in from the pavement, looking about him with the wild expression of someone arriving at a railway station with only half a minute to spare. He caught sight of them and veered over.

"I got terribly held up and then I lost my way," he said breathlessly. "Is it all over?"

"This is Mr. Femmer," Miss Steen explained, grudgingly as it seemed to Richard. His arrival was clearly not to her liking. Turning to Femmer, she said, "This is Mr. Monk, who is Mr. Berg's solicitor."

The two men shook hands.

"I meant to be here by eleven and look at the time now." He shook his head worriedly as his features fell back into their normal melancholy cast.

"You've not missed anything vital," Richard said. "Mr. Berg has been remanded in custody for a week without any evidence being given."

"No, but I ought to have been in court to lend moral support."

"Miss Steen did that," Richard said, and then wondered if it were an altogether tactful remark. "Anyway, you've arrived at an opportune moment as you can join Miss Steen and myself over a cup of coffee. It'll assist me to be able to talk to you both together."

He could tell from her expression that the arrangement displeased her. But this he couldn't help. If she wanted to speak to him alone, there'd be an opportunity later on. Femmer, on the other hand, seemed relieved to find that his arrival was to some purpose after all, and he appeared quite oblivious of her pique.

The coffee-shop to which he led them was newly opened and did a good trade with those released from the court's clutches. More important, its tables were well screened from one another and afforded reasonable privacy. Strange though it might seem this had been done deliberately and was the proprietor's own idea, leading him to call his establishment "The Consultation Room".

Miss Steen lit a cigarette as soon as they were seated and inhaled deeply before directing a fierce jet of smoke at the top of the partition behind Richard's head.

"It's the background of the case I want to ask you about," he said, lowering a spoonful of brown sugar into his cup. "I don't know whether you're aware of the position, but it is going to be alleged that Mr. Berg was involved in spying activities. Not with Russia or any of *her* friends, but with Israel. Did either of you know anything about that?"

"I certainly didn't," Femmer said quickly. "I had no idea. Mr. Berg never gave any hint to me that he was caught up in anything of that sort. Though of course I've not worked in the firm all that long." Miss Steen threw him a look which seemed to spell "Judas", and he added, "I can't believe that Mr. Berg was a traitor in the real sense. He was much too . . . too straight a person. And he certainly wouldn't have done it for money."

"I don't think that'll be suggested."

"How does the dead man come into this? Was he passing stuff to Mr. Berg to pass on to the Israelis?"

"Something like that."

"And why does anyone think it was Mr. Berg who murdered him?" Femmer asked intently.

"Because there was an entry in the dead man's diary purporting to show that he was due to meet Mr. Berg at ten o'clock last Friday night in the public-house outside which the murder took place. That, coupled with a statement Mr. Berg gave the police about his movements that evening which they can prove to be false."

"Oh, no!" Miss Steen said, aghast.

"I'm afraid so."

"I'm not a lawyer, of course," Femmer said, "but that doesn't sound to me to be a very strong case."

"We must hope it doesn't become any stronger," Richard remarked soberly.

"In what way could it become worse for him?" asked Miss Steen.

"It's always possible that the police will unearth further evidence which might seem to point to his guilt. For example, we don't yet know the result of the laboratory examination of his clothing."

"Nobody will ever persuade me that Mr. Berg's killed a man. I wouldn't even believe it if I heard it from his own lips." Her voice held a note of suppressed emotion, and the two men looked at her in silence for a moment.

Femmer said, "That's all very fine and loyal, but hadn't we better stick to facts. I'm sure those are what Mr. Monk is most interested in." He spoke with a quiet firmness and Richard quite expected the reproof to excite a further outburst from Miss Steen, but to his surprise she merely gave a small acquiescing nod and took a gulp of coffee.

"Have either of you heard of the Shraga Shipping Company of Haifa?"

They both shook their heads.

"You've not had any business with a company of that name?"

"No, definitely not," Miss Steen said with seeming reluctance. Monk felt that she regarded the denial as possibly letting down her employer. In fact, of course, everything so far was confirmation of what he had told his solicitor, namely that no one in this country apart from the dead Parsons had known what he was up to.

"Did you know he had a brother living in Israel?"

"Oh, yes, I knew that," she said eagerly. "I used to type letters to him from time to time."

"What sort of letters?"

"Personal letters."

Richard looked at Femmer who said, "I only knew because Miss Steen told me. Mr. Berg never mentioned his brother to me personally."

"There was nothing secret about it," she broke in, as though she'd been accused of betraying her employer's confidence.

"Have either of you heard of the name of Gamel?" Again they shook their heads. Moreover, despite enquiring looks, Richard decided not to enlighten them. They'd learn soon enough, anyway, and meanwhile he didn't wish to get drawn into an explanation of Berg's story. After a silence he said, "What it comes to is this, that when the police question you, as they certainly will, neither of you will be able to tell them anything for the good reason that you didn't know anything." He looked from one to the other and received a nod in reply.

"On the other hand," Femmer said, "and I know I speak for Miss Steen as well, we'd like you to know that we're ready to do absolutely anything to assist Mr. Berg."

"But if you don't know anything, I'm afraid there's nothing you can do."

"You may be able to think of something perhaps, Mr. Monk."

Richard wasn't sure whether this was an offer of perjury or merely a declaration of loyal support. In any event, it came oddly from one who only a few minutes earlier had reproved Miss Steen for her display of emotion.

"All I'm concerned with," he said a trifle stiffly, "is finding out exactly what you know. And it doesn't look as though either of you can give evidence which will assist either the prosecution or the defence."

"Surely, they couldn't make us give evidence for the prosecution anyway, could they?" Miss Steen asked.

"They could indeed. They'd subpoena you, if necessary."

"But how would they know that we'd say what they wanted?"

"If you'd made a statement to the police in the first place and it was of use to the prosecution, they'd subpoena you to attend court and they could apply to treat you as a hostile witness, that is cross-examine you on your statement, if you went as far as retracting what you'd said in it."

"But how could they force one to make a statement in the first place?"

"They couldn't."

"Then I shan't make one," she declared in a forthright tone.

"I wouldn't advise you to do that," he said, "it would only arouse their worst unfounded suspicions and that might react against Mr. Berg." He picked up the bill and reached into his pocket. "I'll be in touch with you again shortly. Meanwhile, I'd like you to let me know at once if you happen to remember any small detail which you think might assist Mr. Berg's defence." He avoided Femmer's eye as he spoke and a few minutes later they separated on the pavement outside.

Richard had been back in his office about half an hour and was dictating a note on the further developments when Sheila shot back into her room to answer the 'phone.

"Miss Steen wants to speak to you," she hissed, putting her head back round the door.

"All right, put her through."

"Mr. Monk?" Elizabeth Steen's voice sounded agitated. "The

police were at the office when we got back. They've taken away a lot of documents and went through a whole lot more."

"Did they produce a warrant?"

"Yes, one issued under the Official Secrets Act. They showed it to Mr. Femmer's secretary."

"What was the name of the officer?"

"There were three of them. The one in charge was a Detective-Inspector Pullar."

"All right, Miss Steen," he said in what he hoped was a calming voice. "Thank you for 'phoning. You can leave the matter with me now."

"There is something else, Mr. Monk."

"Yes?"

"I'd like to speak to you alone as soon as possible. Can I come to your office straightaway now?"

"Very well. You know the address?"

But she had already replaced the receiver.

"I wonder what she's after now," he said in a thoughtful tone, looking at Sheila.

"My job, probably! Seeing how she's lost her own boss!"

7

When Sheila showed Miss Steen into his room about half an hour later, Richard couldn't fail to notice the appraising glances exchanged by the two secretaries. He might not learn what the visitor thought of his secretary, but he had little doubt that it wouldn't require a penny in the slot to find out Sheila's opinion of Miss Steen.

She sat very upright on the edge of his visitor's chair and accepted a cigarette. He reckoned she was somewhere in the early thirties. She had small, neat features which tended, however, to be cowed by a pair of large, soulful eyes. Her hair (she had worn a hat to court, but was now without one) reached to her shoulders and completely framed her face. On the other hand, he realised

61

that the next time he saw her, it would probably be swept up in some elaborate coiffure so that he would have difficulty in recognising her. As far as he was concerned a woman's personality really did change with her hairstyle.

She ran a finger along the top of her shiny, black handbag and appeared absorbed in its progress. When it reached the end, she looked up and said: "I was still suffering a bit from shock when we were in the café and I found it impossible to collect all my thoughts."

"Also you didn't want to talk in front of Mr. Femmer," Richard observed drily.

"Was it very obvious?"

"If he noticed, it didn't seem to worry him."

"It's just that I've been Mr. Berg's secretary for five years and know him better than anyone else does. Patrick Femmer only knows . . . knows his business side." She ran her finger slowly back along the top of the handbag. "I suppose you know that Mr. Berg and his wife don't get on?" Her voice held an aggressive note.

"Does that have anything to do with the present case?"

"I thought you wished to know all the surrounding circumstances."

"All the *relevant* surrounding circumstances, yes."

"Anyway, they didn't," she said flatly. "They haven't done for years."

He had, in fact, guessed this for himself, but it still left him wondering what Miss Steen's object was in telling him.

She made a wry grimace. "You probably ought to know that I've been his mistress for nearly five years.

"Why exactly are you telling me this, Miss Steen?"

"Because you ought to know that I propose to stand by him, even if his wife won't."

"I have no reason to believe that his wife won't stand by him."

"She wasn't at court this morning."

"That doesn't prove anything."

She looked at him in frank surprise, seemed about to say something, but gave an eloquent shrug instead.

"Tell me about these documents which the police have taken possession of."

"All our correspondence dealing with firms in Israel."

"Hmm. Not difficult to guess what they're looking for."

"Surely it's not regarded as spying to pass information to a friendly country like Israel?"

"It most certainly is. It mayn't be as morally serious as spying for the Chinese or the Russians, but legally it's no different. Incidentally, did Mr. Berg ever express any views to you about being a Jew?"

"No, he just accepted it in the same way that you accept being English. At least I imagine you do. He wasn't one of those Jews who feel obligated to tell the world three times a day that they're Jewish. Equally, he certainly wasn't ashamed of being one."

"It doesn't surprise you that he was passing information to Israel?"

"I'm surprised that I didn't know; that's all!" She sounded reproachful. "Mr. Berg and I kept no secrets from one another."

"So you thought, my girl," Richard reflected not without slight relish. "So much for your possessiveness." He always resented, even vicariously, any such suggestion. It seemed an affront to individual dignity and independence. Perhaps this was why he hadn't yet got married.

"Where do you live, Miss Steen?" he asked suddenly.

"I have a small flat in Earl's Court. I live alone."

Her flat couldn't be all that far from the scene of the murder, and it occurred to him that if Berg had given a visit to her as his alibi for Friday evening, the police would presumably have been unable to disprove it. It was inconceivable that she wouldn't have been ready to support a false alibi in her lover's defence. The only reason he could think of for Berg not having done so was to save it coming to his wife's ears.

What a messy domestic set-up it was! Not that it appeared to have any bearing on who stabbed Parsons and for what motive.

"There is something else I think I ought to mention," she said with an obvious effort. "Mr. Berg kept a stiletto paper-knife in the drawer of his desk. It's missing."

"Since when?"

"I can't say."

"Who found it missing?"

"When the police were searching the office, they went through all the drawers of Mr. Berg's desk. They found the sheath in which it was normally kept, and when she saw them examining it, Mr. Femmer's secretary, who was also in the room, without thinking, remarked on the absence of the paper-knife itself." She looked at Richard anxiously. "I wouldn't have mentioned it but for the fact of the police knowing." He could well believe that. "Do you think its disappearance of any importance?" she asked.

"That," he replied, "depends entirely on the circumstances of its reappearance."

8

Over the next two days Richard was busily occupied with the preparation of Berg's defence. He dictated a brief to counsel which gave no indication of the intimacy existing between him and the recipient. It was couched in the formal flowery language of the law and abounded with expressions such as, "counsel is informed", "counsel will no doubt bear in mind" and "counsel will probably take the view". It had always seemed to Richard that the law was richer in euphemisms than any other profession, and use of the third person in communicating with counsel further muffled any sharp edges to the exchange. For example "counsel will no doubt bear in mind" might be translated as, "You're too dumb to think of it for yourself but the important point to remember is . . ." And "counsel will probably take the view" generally meant, "Even *you* must see this. . . ."

In addition to dictating the brief, he visited Berg in prison, and held telephone conversations with Mrs. Berg and Detective-Inspector Pullar. The Special Branch man was non-committal about his examination of the documents seized in Berg's office, though Richard gained the impression that they'd brought him no joy. He found an excuse also to telephone Superintendent Kettleman, and in this instance learnt explicitly that the murder weapon had not so far been found. Kettleman added his own view that now it never would be. To Richard's further question, the Detective-Superintendent had said that the pathologist gave it as his view that the fatal wound could have been caused by any sharp-pointed instrument. Berg himself had been unable to account for the stiletto's disappearance from his office, and Richard had told him not to worry about it.

The other move which he had made toward preparing the defence had been to write to Berg's brother in Israel. It was to an address in Safad which, he was told, was a Galilean hill town where a lot of artists lived. In the letter he told Berg senior that his brother was in serious trouble and awaiting trial for murder, and he asked him to confirm that Joseph Berg had been a mere pawn in whatever the activities had amounted to and that he had not been paid for his services nor had he really been anything more than a post office. He went on to say in the letter that he didn't know whom else to send it to and that he assumed that since Berg senior had originally acted as intermediary he would be able to find out the answers even if they were not immediately in his possession. The letter concluded with a plea for a prompt reply.

It was a long letter and a considerable amount of thought had gone into its drafting since there was no knowing into whose hands it might fall. Hence it was required to impart information, without at the same time giving away anything which might boomerang at Berg. Its composition had not been made any easier by the fact that Berg seemed to be extremely vague about his brother's circumstances. Richard could only hope that the tug of family ties would be enough to bring Berg senior out of the shadows and running to his younger brother's aid. After all, but for him, Joseph Berg would never have become involved, so the least he could now do was to answer the bugle call sounded by Richard's letter.

On Saturday evening Richard went to the Scarbys for dinner. He arrived about half past six after spending a morning at work and an afternoon in a gymnasium, the combined effect of which had produced in him an agreeable sense of well-being.

Alan opened the front door to him, wearing an ancient pair of flannels and a shirt whose original colour had long since gone down the drain in an orgy of detergent.

"Sorry I'm such a mess, Richard, but I've been relaying the kitchen floor with some new patent plastic squares. The job was supposed to be foolproof, but it's turned out worse than one of those ghastly puzzles where you have to fit pieces together to make a square and if you don't do it right . . . well, you have what our kitchen floor now looks like." He glanced into the street just before closing the front door. "I must say your car really adds tone to the district."

"A taxi-driver I met on the corner didn't think so."

Alan grinned. "What happened?"

"We just had a bit of an altercation about who had precedence over the other."

"You won, I hope?"

"I think you could probably best describe it as a draw. I certainly went first, but as I passed him he shouted out, 'I suppose you think you've got a built-in right of way with that bloody great lump of German lard you're driving.'"

Alan laughed. "It is a bit ostentatious for this part of the world. Mind you, I wouldn't mind owning it myself. It's the colour that does it, I suppose. If it were black, nobody would notice it twice, but white cars, rather like white cats, are apt to draw attention to themselves. Can't see anyone stealing it to use on a raid." He led Richard into the living-room, picking his way across a floor littered with toys. He put his toe beneath a pink rabbit and deftly converted it on to the sofa.

"Jane's putting the infant to bed. When she comes down, I'll go and tidy myself up. Meanwhile, what'll it be, sherry, Cinzano or . . . or nothing. I'm afraid that's the lot within your range."

"I'll have a plain Cinzano."

"I was reading the brief you sent me on Berg," Alan went on as he poured out the drinks. "What struck me was that even if Gamel can't be traced in time, we must do everything we can to authenticate his existence. It's vital that the jury are made to accept him as a real person of flesh and blood and not as a misty creation who may or may not exist. Unless we can satisfy them that he is a very real person, we're going to be up against it. If they ever think Gamel is an invention, it's but a short step to their convicting our chap, since there could be only one explanation of inventing him."

"I hope he's going to be found," Richard said, taking a sip at his drink.

"So do I, but if he's not, then I'm afraid you'll have to take proofs from everyone who can testify to his existence and to his disappearance since the murder."

"The police accept that he exists. Certainly the Special Branch do."

"Maybe, but they don't accept that he had anything to do with the murder. We have got to be able to satisfy the jury not only that he exists, but that he has disappeared because he's the murderer." He paused and looked thoughtful. "If we could be sure of bringing that off, I'd much sooner Gamel never did turn up. I don't know whether you've thought about it, Richard, but his reappearance could prove a liability. I mean, if he denies complicity in the murder and can establish some sort of alibi, it's going to turn into a slogging match between him and our chap, with the jury all the time having at the back of their minds that it's Berg who has been charged and not Gamel."

"When you've met Berg, Alan, I think you'll believe his story."

"It doesn't make any difference whether I do or not. Sometimes one can't avoid making up one's mind about the truth of a client's defence, but speaking for myself I've never found it helped me as an advocate to believe in the cause I'm paid to plead. Advocates who became personally indentified with their clients' cases are apt to be an emotional pain in the neck."

"To hear you talk, one would never think you were a devoted husband and an adoring father. You sound like that pontificating old bore, Dr. Johnson himself."

"He had a point. However, I bet he never laid any floors in his life. Nor, of course, have you! You're the sort of person who'd ring up Harrods to send a man to change an electric light bulb."

"What rubbish!" Richard said in an amused but not very convincing tone. "Anyway, I can't see much virtue in having a kitchen floor looking like something salvaged from Pompeii. I remember you never were much good at geometry."

During the next few minutes they amused themselves reminiscing about their mathematics master at school whom each had cordially disliked. Then Jane Scarby came into the room.

She was tall and blonde and had been a moderately successful model before marrying Alan, a profession, she was fond of reminding him, more competitive than his own.

Richard jumped up as she entered and they kissed.

"How delicious you smell, Jane!"

"It's baby powder. But thank you all the same."

She had a pair of the clearest blue eyes he had ever seen, which would have been the reason he would have married her if he had given the matter serious thought.

She sat down on the sofa and lay back, managing, Richard thought, to look natural and elegant at the same time.

"Give me a drink, darling, before I go and get dinner."

Alan handed her a gin and tonic and said to Richard, "I don't know whether you realise it, but we always have a five-star dinner when you come."

"Jane's incapable of anything less."

"You miss the point. I know my wife's a superlative cook, but only when she wants to be. The thing is she can't always be bothered, but your presence puts her on her mettle."

"You mean because I'm a pretty good cook myself?"

"Fairly if immodestly put."

Jane who had been listening with an air of relaxed amusement now said, "That Boeuf Strogonoff you gave us the other night, Richard, really was delicious. It's an awful shame you've not married. Think what some girl is missing."

Richard grinned. "Every bachelor needs to have his gimmick. Mine's cooking. The secret being a small, highly selective repertoire of exotic dishes, which are fun to do. If you ever ask for bacon and eggs in my flat, I'll take you out to the nearest Lyons."

"Or fry them yourself in Devonshire cream and a pint of vintage claret," Alan murmured amiably, "with chopped tarragon sprinkled on before serving."

"Listen to this from the man whose boiled eggs would make good insides for golf balls," Jane said, finishing her drink and getting up.

"You know that's not fair. The clock stopped," her husband observed.

Jane looked across at Richard and said with a laugh, "And not only the clock. Practically life itself stops when Alan's set loose in the kitchen."

About an hour later, the three of them sat back after coq au vin followed by fresh fruit salad.

"That was delicious, Jane," Richard said appreciatively.

"Yes, darling, it really was," Alan added. "I shan't need

another meal until Richard invites us again. You have a rest and I'll get the coffee."

A few seconds later there was a loud pop and a strangulated oath. "He can't even light the gas stove without practically blowing up the house," Jane said affectionately. She lit a cigarette and leant back with a sigh of comfort. "He was telling me about this case you've just sent him. It sounds interesting."

"It is. Also I've taken rather a fancy to Berg."

"You really think he's innocent?"

"Yes, I believe he is."

"But you could be wrong?"

"Certainly. After five years of criminal practice, one realises that one can always be wrong in matters affecting human conduct. The only predictable thing about human nature is its unpredictability."

"I wonder if that's really so," Jane said thoughtfully.

"I'm sure of it."

"But I can think of lots of people I know whose behaviour is utterly predictable in given circumstances."

"I grant you they may be predictable so far as social conventions go. For example one will be embarrassed by this, another made angry by that. You're sure of it and the odds are you'll be right. But the point is that you don't really know anyone. You don't really know Alan and Alan doesn't really know you. There's no such thing as a simple person, even though certain stupid people are rather fond of claiming it in respect of themselves. Each of us is vastly complex. Very often we don't know ourselves, so how much less can anyone else know us. *Really* know us. It's impossible. It's beyond the realms of human communication. For the moment I'm inclined to accept what Berg has told me, but I shan't be surprised if I find that I've been deceived. After all, *he* deceived his wife. He tells me that she had no idea he was involved in this spying business and she confirms it."

"What you're really saying, Richard, is that human nature holds no further surprises for you."

"That's about it. I'm not saying that I'm not capable of being shocked and appalled and stunned by its manifestations. But surprised, no. For example you might be shocked if you suddenly learnt that I was the brains behind the train robbery, but you oughtn't to be surprised."

"Frankly, I'd be thrilled. Were you, incidentally?"

"No."

"I believe you're deceiving me, Richard."

"On this occasion, not."

"How can I be sure?"

"You can't."

Alan returned to the room, carrying a tray. "What on earth have you been talking about? Bits kept on floating out to the kitchen, but I couldn't make head or tail of it."

"Richard was just saying that he'd never be surprised to learn that you were a back-street abortionist," Jane said, blithely.

The two of them burst into laughter at Alan's astonished expression before she went on to explain the theme which Richard had been developing.

"No wonder he's never got married," Alan remarked at the end.

Discussion came back to the Berg case, and Jane listened while the two men exchanged views on the best tactics to adopt in furtherance of his defence.

During a pause in the conversation, she said, "I must say you manage to make the whole criminal process sound just like a game. Moreover, the sort of game which only the British, with their obsession about fair play, could have devised."

"It's none the worse for that," Alan observed. "A sense of fair play must lie at the root of all justice."

"But do the rules of the game enable a court really to ascertain the truth?" Jane asked. "It seems to me that their main object is to ensure that the accused is not found guilty as a result of a foul by the other side. They're designed, in fact, to protect him against foul play, not to assist in digging out all the truth of a matter. If you can't prove him guilty within the rules, then he goes free, even though he may be guilty."

"Very right and proper, too," her husband said firmly.

"Well, is it? I should have thought it was in society's interest that guilty people were convicted as often as possible. Hearing you two talk, it's obvious that a great number get off. This may be fine for your reputations, but is it so good for society?"

"Far better," Alan said, "that a hundred guilty men should be acquitted than that one innocent person should be convicted."

"I've heard that one before," Jane said sardonically. "I know it's one of the proud planks on which British justice is built, but even though it's heresy to say so I think it's a piece of starry-eyed hypocrisy. I'd far sooner think that the hundred guilty men ended up in prison and let the one innocent take his chance. If he finishes up there too, it'll probably be his own fault and it'll make him more careful next time. I shan't weep for him."

For a few seconds the two men continued looking at her in silence. Finally, Alan said, "Thank God, darling, there's no chance of your ever being on the jury in any of my cases."

"I agree that the whole thing is out of balance these days," Richard said. "The crooks get smarter all the time and the rules are all in their favour. It must be extremely frustrating for the police."

"All because of the obsession about fair play and helping the under-dog," Jane said in a challenging tone.

"You could argue that the police are the under-dogs," Richard murmured, "though I doubt whether the public at large is yet ready to concede that."

"It's all very well knocking fair play," Alan broke in vigorously, "but for all you say, it's still the great strength of the administration of justice in this country and a bloody good thing too. I know I'd sooner be tried under our system than any other."

"You mean if you were guilty?" Jane enquired.

"If I were innocent or guilty."

"Well, naturally you would, you'd have a far better chance of getting off either way than under most other systems." She gave a small laugh. "Listen to me talking as the great expert on the workings of the criminal law. All I know about our own system is enshrined in a few adages one learnt at school—and picked up from a husband and his legal friends."

Richard grinned. "You mayn't know it, but you've made out a very good case for the inquisitorial, as opposed to the accusatorial, system."

"Which is ours?"

"Accusatorial. Most continental systems are the other. Incidentally, after all this lego-philosophical discussion, supposing you were on the Berg jury, what would your verdict be?"

"Depends what sort of an impression he made on me. What sort of an impression the witnesses on the other side made, too."

"Impression! Impression!" Alan said severely. "Verdicts are reached on evidence, not on impressions."

"If you really believed that," Richard remarked, "you'd never need to make final speeches to juries."

"Not even ones with women on them," Jane added. She turned to Richard. "If I believed your Mr. Berg, then naturally I wouldn't find him guilty, however much the evidence might point against him. But if I thought he couldn't be believed, then as far as I'm concerned he'd have had it."

"But I've already told you he's lied to the police about his movements. He's going to have to admit that to the jury. Do you think, as a juror, you could still believe him when he says he didn't murder Parsons?"

"It comes back to impressions, doesn't it, Richard? Not what he says but the manner in which he says it."

Richard nodded. "I think so, too. Coupled with what develops over the Gamel situation. He could make or break us."

It was after midnight when he took his leave of the Scarbys and drove home. It had been the sort of relaxed and comfortable evening he enjoyed most. And the coq au vin really had been excellent. Now he'd have to learn some new dish before they came to dinner with him again. Perhaps he'd try a soufflé, with a standby in case it proved a disaster.

He was still thinking about the soufflé as he closed his front door behind him. His thoughts, however, were rudely shattered by the telephone which immediately began ringing as if it had been impatiently awaiting his return. As he walked into the living-room to take the call it occurred to him that it was making rather a habit of doing this.

"Richard Monk speaking," he announced in unenthusiastic tones.

"You don't know me, Mr. Monk, but I have some advice for you."

The voice had a slightly muffled sound, but was harsh in tone and bore traces of a foreign accent.

"Who is that speaking?"

"Let's say that I am a friend of Mr. Gamel."

"Where is Mr. Gamel now?" Richard broke in.

But the voice ignored the interruption and went on, "Mr. Monk, I must advise you to forget about Mr. Gamel. Mr. Berg killed Mr. Parsons and looking for Mr. Gamel won't help you."

He might have been referring to three Civil Service colleagues with his meticulous use of 'Mr.'

"You can't expect me to accept advice from an anonymous caller. Who are you?"

"It doesn't matter who I am, the advice is still good."

"How do I know you're a friend of Mr. Gamel?"

"You must take my word for it, Mr. Monk."

"Can I get in touch with you again somehow?" Richard asked, urgently. He felt he had to keep the man talking in the hope of gleaning something useful, of gathering a clue for the future.

The man gave a short, harsh laugh. "No, you cannot, Mr. Monk. It's up to you whether you accept my advice or not. But if you're sensible, you will do so."

"You tell me to forget about Mr. Gamel, but how do you know of my interest in him in the first place?" Richard asked, with a note of sudden excited triumph in his voice.

"You have not read the evening papers?" the man enquired with some surprise.

"What about the evening papers?"

"The statement by Scotland Yard? You've not seen it?"

"I haven't seen a paper this evening."

"Or listened to the news on the radio?"

"No. I've no idea what statement you're talking about."

"Scotland Yard wants to find Mr. Gamel and have asked for any information as to his whereabouts."

"And what makes you think this announcement is of special interest to me?"

"You are not being very clever, Mr. Monk. Shall I just say that a chain has many links! Mr. Berg and Mr. Parsons and Mr. Gamel were only three of the links in a particular chain. And now I've said all I have to say. . . ."

"Just before you ring off. . . ."

"Good night, Mr. Monk."

A second later the line went dead. Putting down the receiver Richard dashed across to the window. He was just in time to see a figure slip out of the telephone kiosk a hundred yards along the road and disappear round the corner.

So the mysterious Mr. Gamel had friends! Or could the caller even have been Mr. Gamel himself?

9

Detective-Superintendent Kettleman looked up slowly through a veil of drifting cigarette smoke as Inspector Evans came into his office. He had been reading one of his subordinate's reports in a case of alleged rape and been wondering how he was going to minute the file.

"Have a chair," he said moodily. He glanced back at the file. "Know anything about this fellow Wright? Sergeant Baxter's all for charging him with rape."

"I've heard Ted Baxter talking about it. I gather you don't agree with him, sir?"

"In my young days rape meant something really vicious and nasty. Nowadays, it's just an afterthought on the part of the girl. In this case, a little eighteen-year-old chit of a thing alleges that the boy *she* picked up in the Purple Highwayman Club drove her up on to the common and raped her in the back of his mini van. Twenty-four hours later, when her father was bawling her out for coming in late, she burst into tears and said she'd been raped, and along they all come to the police station."

"I take it the chap says she consented?"

"He practically says she seduced him."

"Why does Sergeant Baxter think it's a case then?"

"Search me! He says he thinks she'll make a good witness." His tone was scornful.

"Any medical evidence?"

"To the effect that the girl lost her virginity about the same time as her baby teeth." He sighed. "Ah, well, I suppose I'd better have a word with Baxter. Probably find he thought our crime statistics needed a boost."

Inspector Evans gave a faint smile. "I only looked in to ask, sir, if you want me at court tomorrow in Berg?"

"No need for you to come. I'll have to be there to ask for another remand, but nothing's going to happen."

"What do you make of this anonymous 'phone call his solicitor received on Saturday night?"

Kettleman grimaced. "Could have been anyone! Could even have been a crank!"

"Still no sign of Gamel."

"If it weren't for Special Branch, I'd doubt his existence. However, if they say so, I suppose there must be such a person."

"Though not necessarily connected with this case."

"He mayn't have anything to do with it at all. But that's why we've got to find him if we can. Without him, the defence are going to have a fine old time trailing red herrings hither and thither." He pursed his lips and looked thoughtful. "Though, personally, I think we have quite a strong case against Master Berg. He's lied about his movements at the crucial time, and what's more it sounds as if he's going to have to admit it. And the jury's not going to like that. We have that diary entry, and moreover, we can suggest a motive. Also we can even prove that the murder was committed with the sort of weapon to which he had access and which has disappeared from his office. I don't suppose we'll ever find it now, but it's a bit more to throw into the scales against him." He squinted down his nose at the desk. "No, I think we've got quite a good case." He raised his head suddenly. "Don't you?"

"Yes, I think we have, sir. Furthermore, I'm sure he did it."

"Of course he did it. You don't tell lies to the police unless you have something to hide. And what else has he to hide than that he killed Parsons? Oh, no, he did it all right. The fact that he seems quite a nice bloke doesn't mean a thing. Most of my murderers have been a thoroughly decent lot. There've been exceptions, but on the whole the murderers are the best of the criminal bunch, wouldn't you say?"

Inspector Evans nodded. "Definitely. And they usually give less trouble than all the other types."

"Hmm! I'm not so sure that applies to Berg," Kettleman observed morosely. After a pause he went on, "We did well to obtain that quick statement from his wife. Even though we can't call her as a witness, she's now tied down to saying that her husband told her he was going to meet a business friend that evening. She can't go into the box for the defence and spin a different tale, without being completely discredited in cross-examination."

Inspector Evans looked doubtful. "I can't conceive that she'd be likely to in this case."

"Perhaps not. But you never know what wives won't get up to to assist their husbands."

"But he *was* going to meet a business friend in one sense," Inspector Evans persisted.

"Not in the sense his wife understood," Kettleman replied with finality. He now realised that he had spoken hastily and was glad to clamber back along the limb which had been beginning to creak ominously beneath him. Senior officers could afford to admit mistakes of fact. What they couldn't do without humiliation was reveal basic misconceptions of the facts, which had been Kettleman's danger in the recent exchange. He now saw the complete unlikelihood of Mrs. Berg ever wanting to depart from the terms of the statement she had already made. There was no question of her husband wanting her to help him establish an alibi. On the contrary, there was every reason for thinking that he was in the process of dismantling one. One, moreover, which didn't rest on his wife's evidence in the first place.

"Are you a betting man, Hugh?" Kettleman enquired abruptly.

"Why do you ask, sir?" Evans's tone was suspicious.

"I wondered if you'd care to place a bet on the probability of Berg's conviction. I'll give you eight to one in half-crowns."

"I accept that." A slow smile spread across the inspector's face. "Purely as a betting man of course."

10

Elizabeth Steen sat typing a letter to her employer in prison. The first page was taken up with business details and she had reached the stage where she wanted to add something which would convey to him some of the pent-up emotion she was feeling. Something which would bring him comfort, as well as remind him of her devoted loyalty. But she wasn't finding it easy to express her feelings in words, still less in words which would presumably be read by others and might even be put to some unscrupulous use, she supposed, if she weren't sufficiently careful. She wasn't very clear how this could come about, but a basic sense told her that letters sent to people in prison should be cautious to the point of innocuous.

It was now a week since Mr. Berg had been arrested, but not one telephone call had his wife made to the office to find out how the business was faring. For all she cared, it might have disappeared down one of London's sewers. Though she'd learn soon enough if the profits dried up.

Not for the first time, Beth Steen reflected on the core of gnawing frustration round which her life had grown these past few years. To be in love with a man who accepted you as his mistress, but didn't want you for his wife. Except that she could normally persuade herself that he would marry her one day. The trouble was he was too considerate, he shrank from hurting his wife, even though a complete break would be kinder to everyone in the end. How often she had tried to hint at this, without actually expressing it explicitly. There was nothing more demoralising than to experience insecurity, and at the moment she felt very insecure.

She began tapping at the typewriter keys again.

"I shall post this letter to you today, even though I hope to see you at court tomorrow. . . ."

Her door opened quietly and Femmer came in. He looked at her with his rather mournful expression and she stared back in silence. She liked him, and he had been really wonderful in the office this past week. He was the person who had kept the business going. Of course she'd been there to guide him when necessary, but he already knew as much about its intricacies as she did after five years.

"Will you be going to court tomorrow, Beth?" he asked. He had suggested two days earlier that they should get on christian name terms and she had, to her subsequent surprise, readily agreed.

"Yes, I shall definitely be going."

"I don't suppose Mr. Berg will mind if I'm not there, but I want to clinch that deal with Moores of Wolverhampton. The managing director is coming to town tomorrow and I'm pretty sure I'll be able to satisfy him about terms and conclude arrangements."

"Mr. Berg'll be very pleased about that, Patrick. It was one of the deals he'd set his heart on bringing off."

"Well, I think it's as good as in the bag. I've had the managing director on the 'phone this morning and he sounded delighted with what I was able to tell him." A silence fell between them before Femmer said in a reflective tone, "The British are a funny people! Do you know that only one out of all our customers has referred directly to Mr. Berg being charged with murder. He made some crack about conducting our business from the dock of the Old Bailey. All the others have either avoided all mention of it or have used the sort of euphemisms one murmurs to people who have suffered bereavements." He strolled across to the window and looked out on the busy street below with a distant view of the roof of Liverpool Street Station. "And now I come to think of it," he added, addressing the pane of glass, "that one was only naturalised British, so he doesn't count." He turned round and gave Beth Steen a look of amused despair.

"It wouldn't be in very good taste for comparative strangers to refer to the firm's current misfortunes."

Femmer's expression became one of undisguisable amusement. "I'm sorry, Beth," he said, "but you sound just like them, talking about good taste and the firm's current misfortunes." He walked over to her. "You must forgive my unseemly sense of the absurd," he said in a disarming tone.

For a second or two, he thought she was going to reprove him, but then she also smiled.

"I'm sure Mr. Berg would find it amusing, too. He can always see the ridiculous side of a situation."

"I've been wondering if you would like to go out with me one evening, Beth," he said suddenly. She looked up to find him watching her intently.

"Yes, I think I should, Patrick."

"Only think?"

"No, I should."

"What about tomorrow then?"

"Well . . . yes."

"That's fine. I'll come and pick you up at your place. Will seven o'clock be all right?"

"I'll be ready."

He went out of the room, leaving her staring vacantly at the half-written letter in her typewriter.

Hilda Berg shut the front door and felt for the hall light. Then she went into the drawing-room and poured herself a brandy and ginger ale. It was a quarter to midnight and she meant to go to bed as soon as she had finished her drink.

She had been surprised to find how quickly she had become used to having the house to herself. Not emotionally surprised, but with a clinical interest in the discovery.

Opening her handbag, she took out the letter she had received from her husband. It had been written in prison the day after his first appearance in court and she had already read it several times. She now did so again.

"My dear Hilda," it ran, "I'm afraid my arrest must have come as a great shock to you and I'm sorry about that. I have told the police that you knew nothing and I shall do my best to ensure that you are caused the minimum of bother. Certainly I shall do nothing to add to your difficulties. Which brings me to the matter of your visiting me here. I hope you will agree that it will be much better for both of us if you don't. I imagine we should both be embarrassed. I know I should. What I'm trying to say, of course, is that since we've reached the end of the road, it would be better to recognise the fact. Acquitted or convicted I can only be a further embarrassment to you, and I have no doubt that you'll be able to get a divorce somehow. I'll do nothing to prevent it. Finally, I'll see that you continue to be provided for. Now, I'll say good-bye. Joe."

She refolded the letter and returned it to her handbag. If he really intended she should divorce him, she wondered why he hadn't offered to provide her with the necessary evidence. She felt pretty certain he could do so if he wanted. Not that she was particularly troubled over the matter, she merely wondered why he hadn't been more explicit in his letter. Her intuition had long ago told her that he was being unfaithful and she'd assumed it was his secretary. Those large soulful eyes and the neck full of cords vibrating with neurosis. If ever there was a suppressed nymphomaniac, it was she!

But for his letter she would, of course, have been to visit him. As it was, however, she was relieved to have been absolved from the obligation. It could, as he said, have been only an awkward occasion for both them. Now she could tell her curious friends and acquaintances that Joe had specially asked her not to go and see him and she'd decided to respect his wish.

Be the truth told, the great majority of her friends had behaved in much the same way as the firm's customers had toward Patrick Femmer. They had murmured words of sympathy appropriate to a sudden bereavement and then quickly gone on to behave as if nothing untoward had happened at all. Only one had taken her aside after bridge the previous evening and enquired eagerly if she could ensure her a seat at the trial; and she was someone who was obsessed with the seamier details of her own two divorce actions and never tired of giving a blow by blow description of them. She collected court dramas, her own and other peoples, and hoarded them in the somewhat unattractive store-room of her mind.

Hilda Berg finished her drink and rose to go up to bed. She was a patient woman and was quite prepared to wait and see how things turned out.

She had stripped her husband's bed of its sheets and blankets and now it was covered only with a dark green spread, not unlike a funeral bier in appearance.

She thought she'd probably take the bed to bits and put it away in the box-room. It would give her much more space. She drifted off into a peaceful sleep while mentally rearranging the bedroom furniture.

11

Richard arrived at court soon after ten the next morning and went straight to the jailer's office.

"Can I go and see Berg?"

" 'Fraid the van's not come yet, Mr. Monk," the jailer said, buttoning up his tunic, which had been made for a slimmer man. "Should be here any minute, though."

Five minutes later the van, which did a milk-round dropping off prisoners at their respective courts, pulled into the yard and disgorged its candidates for Mr. Chaplin's attention.

Berg was looking calmer and altogether more relaxed when Richard saw him. It was invariably so; prison seemed to achieve a therapeutic effect on those remanded in custody.

"Hello, Mr. Monk. Any news?"

Richard told him of the telephone call he had received a few nights before. "Any idea who it could have been?" he asked.

A worried frown creased Berg's face. Slowly he shook his head. "Absolutely none. Do you think it might have been Gamel himself?"

"The possibility had entered my mind."

"Have you told the police?"

"Yes." Noticing Berg's anxious expression he went on, "No harm done by informing them. It doesn't strengthen their case against you, and on one view it shows that there is someone at large who is hoping to see you convicted."

"When will the case actually start?" Berg asked, after digesting what Richard had told him.

"They're going to fix a date next week."

"Good. The sooner the better. And how long will it be after that before the trial takes place?"

"About three weeks. If a trial is ordered."

"How do you mean?"

"The magistrate first has to be satisfied that you have a case to answer."

"Isn't that a foregone conclusion?"

"Who told you that?"

"It's what I've heard in Brixton."

"Well, it's not strictly true. Admittedly some magistrates are more easily satisfied than others, but none of them would commit for trial on no evidence."

"You can't say there's no evidence against me."

"Let's wait and hear the prosecution case," Richard said firmly. "I can assure you that Mr. Scarby will make a submission of no case to answer if he thinks it has the slightest chance of success. Incidentally, I'll introduce you to him after your appearance this morning."

He emerged into the court vestibule just as Alan came through the swing doors.

" 'Morning, Richard." He looked uncommonly cheerful. "I've parked my car just behind yours. I thought it might help to disabuse the public of the popular notion that it's barristers who make all the money and solicitors who work away like unpaid Cinderellas. Perhaps we could arrange for a press photograph when we're leaving."

Richard looked his friend up and down. As always, he was extremely well dressed. He not only had a good figure, but managed to wear his clothes so that they looked natural as well as smart. For court, he invariably wore a black jacket and striped trousers. Where most men's ties behaved like recalcitrant snakes, Alan's always remained neatly knotted. Where their shoes were down at heel or turned up at toe, Alan's gave the appearance of being packed with trees rather than feet. Two of the pockets in his waistcoat were linked by a thin gold chain which helped to emphasise the boardlike flatness of his stomach.

Richard allowed his gaze to fasten on the gold chain.

"By all means," he said. "Except who's going to believe the Merc. is not yours." He glanced down at himself. The black knitted tie visibly restive, the trousers in need of a press, and the dark suede shoes looking as though he'd just come in from the Sahara. In fact, it was whitewash off Berg's cell wall which had somehow got on to them. "It'll be like one of those newspaper competitions where you have to pair objects off. You'd certainly be paired with the Mercedes and I with the battered Ford Zephyr."

"Just shows how misleading appearances can be," Alan said lightly, slipping the piece of pink tape off his brief and hanging it over his wrist.

"Good morning, Mr. Monk."

Richard turned to find Miss Steen at his elbow. She was wearing an apricot coloured suit and her hair was tucked away under a fur hat which seemed in danger of suddenly enveloping her whole head.

Richard introduced her to Alan who gave her a look of interested appraisal.

"Have you seen Mr. Berg this morning?" she asked.

"Yes."

"Do you think it would be possible for me to see him afterwards?" She observed his dubious expression and, interpreting it aright, added, "That is, if Mrs. Berg doesn't show up."

Richard looked enquiringly at Alan.

"I don't see why we shouldn't ask the magistrate for Miss Steen to be allowed to see him," Alan said in a judicial tone. "After all, she is his secretary and helping to keep his business running and they must have things to discuss in that connection."

"Will you ask him then, Mr. Scarby?"

"Certainly, I'll make the application. Provided the police have no objection, I'm sure the magistrate won't."

"The only thing is," Richard said, "you were going to see him afterwards."

"I'm sure Miss Steen won't mind waiting," Alan observed blandly. "I shan't want more than ten minutes with him."

"No, of course," she replied. "I'm not in any hurry to get away."

Mr. Chaplin had begun his morning's work when they entered the court-room, and the lawyers' pew was well filled. However, Richard and Alan managed to squeeze in at one end of the row to the petulant murmurings of a large, flabby·solicitor who had an office directly opposite the court and who considered that this gave him proprietary rights.

Mr. Chaplin surveyed the scene with his customary dispassion and uttered the minimum of words to keep the court's business moving.

When Berg's case was called on, Alan rose and announced that he now appeared on behalf of the defendant. Mr. Chaplin nodded his acknowledgement of this information which he already had anyway.

Richard turned round to give Berg a small smile of encouragement, but Alan studiously avoided doing so. As he remarked afterwards, "I always think it's rather rude to turn and stare at one's client before one's even met him."

Detective-Superintendent Kettleman stepped into the witness-box and gripping the sides as though he expected it to try to buck he asked for a further remand in custody.

"Will you be ready to go on next week, Superintendent?" Alan asked, after Mr. Chaplin had transmitted one of his silent cues.

"The file is now with the Director of Public Prosecutions and I understand he'll be ready by then."

"I've set aside the whole of next Wednesday for this case," Mr. Chaplin said briskly, and made a quick entry in his register. "Meanwhile, you'll be remanded in custody."

Alan remembered just in time to ask if his client's secretary might visit him in the cells and Mr. Chaplin, after glancing at Kettleman, nodded.

A further nod indicated that they were all dismissed. Outside the court-room, one of the reporters came up to them.

"Don't tell me if you don't want to," he said with an empty smile, "but is your chap putting up an alibi?"

"I'm afraid I can't tell you that," Alan replied.

"Can't or won't?"

"Won't."

"Fair enough," the man said, his smile still intact. "What are your hopes of finding Gamel do you think?"

"Surely you mean the police hopes? It's they who are looking for him."

"But *you* who want him?"

"We're naturally interested in the result of the search."

"The Press are doing their best for you. We really can help on occasions like this. There can't be anyone who's able to read who isn't aware of the search for Gamel. Personally, I believe he's out of the country. I think he probably got away within a matter of hours of the murder being committed."

Alan grinned. "You chaps always know far more than anyone else."

"We have better sources of information than most. I bet I know more about the background of this case than either of you."

"Very likely."

"More even than the police."

"I wouldn't dispute it."

"For example, did you know that the dead man had been in prison?"

"When?"

"I thought that might interest you."

"You're right, it does."

"A long while ago. He was only in his early twenties at the time. He got three months for forging a postal draft. It was up in Liverpool." His tone became more button-holing. "Tell you a funny thing about the case, too. He forged the name of the old man to whom the draft had been sent and who died that same day. It was a Friday and one of the local papers ran a headline about 'The case of the man who died on Friday'. Curious, isn't it?"

84

"Not particularly," Alan said, with rapidly dying interest.

"But now Parsons is the man who died on Friday."

"Lots of people die on Fridays," Richard observed. "As many as on any other day of the week, I imagine."

The newpaper man looked at him sadly. "You'd be no good writing for the popular Press. A legal training has eroded your imagination. Now, all the case needs is for something else to happen on a Friday. . . . "

"Come on, Richard," Alan broke in. "We must go and see Berg or he'll think we've forgotten him."

"Wonder what paper he's on," Richard said as they walked toward the jailer's office.

"Not *The Times*, anyway," Alan remarked drily.

As his cell door was unlocked, Berg jumped up as though welcoming cocktail guests.

"This is Mr. Scarby," Richard said.

"I saw you in court, of course," Berg said, shaking his counsel's hand. "Though back view only, I'm afraid."

"In some courts, defendants sit at the bottom of a well and can only see the roof. I suppose something of what goes on may drift down to them."

"I imagine courts are designed to suit the lawyers rather than the prisoners," Berg remarked with a faint smile.

"If you really want to know, Mr. Berg, the old ones were designed to ensure that no one could do anything in any comfort, either stand up or sit down, or get in and out. The new ones to fulfil some architect's conception of what a court *should* be like. In both cases, the result, though different to look at, is much the same." He removed his brief from beneath his arm. "However, let's now talk about your case. . . . "

For the next ten minutes or so, Alan asked questions and Berg answered. Richard, who leant against the cell door listening, heard nothing which he hadn't heard before. He knew Alan's intention was primarily to meet his client and sum him up, not to learn anything new. Until counsel could form an assessment of a client, he couldn't know what sort of a witness he would make and how well he would stand up to cross-examination.

"I don't think I have anything further to ask Mr. Berg, Richard," he said at length. "Have you got any points?"

"There is one small matter," Richard said, looking at Berg.

"As I told you, I wrote to your brother six days ago. How soon do you think I ought to get a reply?"

"You should hear from him within the next three or four days. Certainly by the middle of next week. He always answers letters promptly."

"Good. And, of course, I did stress the urgency."

"There's something I'd like to ask before you two gentlemen leave," Berg said.

"Sure, go ahead," Alan replied.

"Is it right that my wife can't be called as a witness?"

"Not by the prosecution."

"That's what I meant."

"Yes, its quite right. She is what the law calls neither competent nor compellable. We can call her for the defence, of course."

Berg shook his head. "There's nothing she can say."

12

Mrs. Cluff placed her hot-water bottle into the bulging suit-case and glanced round the room to make sure she'd left nothing behind. Then, closing the lid, she locked the case and put on her hat and coat.

As always she had enjoyed staying with her sister, but now she was quite ready to go home. After ten days in the country, she found herself missing the hum of London life. Not that she led a gay existence, but she missed the neighbourhood's familiar sounds and smells, and the people she'd meet in the shops every day. Here in Norfolk the only sounds you heard were birds, and an occasional cow and high-flying jet bomber. Moreover, there was only one shop in her sister's village, and a weekly pilgrimage into Fakenham was no substitute for having the butcher and the baker and the grocer just round the corner at the bottom of your road.

"I'm all packed and ready, dear," she said to her sister as she carried her suitcase downstairs.

"You needn't leave for another ten minutes. The bus is always a few minutes late."

"I hope I shan't miss my train."

"You should have lots of time. But, if you do, you must just come back for the night."

Mrs. Cluff grimaced. "Once I'm packed, I'm ready to go," she said forthrightly.

"I hope you'll find everything all right when you get back," her sister said in a tone full of doubt.

"And why shouldn't I?"

"Well, I mean, just leaving the place to your lodger, anything may have happened, particularly as he's a foreigner."

"He's much more of a gentleman than some of the English lodgers I've had."

Her sister accepted this statement with obvious reservation. "What did you say his name was?"

"Mr. Fawzi."

"Is he very dark-skinned?" her sister asked in the same tone she might have used to enquire whether he suffered from leprosy.

"He's an Egyptian," Mrs. Cluff replied, with the implication that this provided an adequate description of her lodger's physiognomy.

"Well, I hope you'll find everything all right," her sister repeated, her doubts seemingly reinforced rather than dissipated. "I think we ought to make a move now, dear, the bus is never very late. . . ."

It was just after half past six when Mrs. Cluff opened her front door and stepped briskly across the threshold. She put down her suitcase and wrinkled her nose as she breathed in her first lungful of home air. It smelt curiously stale and musty. Mr. Fawzi couldn't have bothered to open any windows while she was away. She felt inside the letter-box and was surprised to find it almost full. Presumably he'd been taking his letters and leaving hers there. Well, perhaps he hadn't liked to touch them, she thought. Anyway, she was sure the cause was good manners rather than neglect. This was borne out when she discovered that all the letters in the box were, indeed, addressed to her. It did just flick across her mind that he hadn't received any mail during the month he had been her lodger, but she'd assumed that this was only because he hadn't yet had time to receive any letters from his family and friends in Egypt. Or rather the United Arab Republic, as he had politely but firmly reminded her on more than one occasion.

The same stale smell pervaded the kitchen. The sink was bone dry, apart from a small wet patch beneath the cold tap which dripped with the regularity of a barely moving metronome. From one side of the patch there was a snail's trail of moisture toward the plug hole.

Returning to the hall, Mrs. Cluff picked up her suitcase and started upstairs.

As her head came level with the floor above, she glanced through the landing railings and felt a sudden tingling of unmistakable apprehension. Till this moment she hadn't really believed that anything was wrong, but now as her gaze fell upon the teacup outside his bedroom door, alarm seized her.

It was not the mere presence of the teacup just where she had placed it at half past seven on the Saturday morning of her departure, but the fact that she could see it was still full. A cold, greasy scum covered the top, and beneath the saucer lay the note which she had left for him giving her address in Norfolk and the exact date of her return.

She held her breath and thought hard for a moment. It was now beyond doubt that something had happened to Mr. Fawzi. Her immediate instinct was to go straight back downstairs and telephone the police from the call-box on the corner. After a further second, however, she mounted the remaining stairs to the top and cautiously tried the handle of his door, averting her gaze from the cup and saucer sitting so ominously at her feet.

The door was locked.

This time she did go out and telephone the police.

Within five minutes, a police patrol car turned into the street where Mrs. Cluff lived and pulled up outside her door. Two flat-capped officers got out and one of them put his finger firmly on the bell-push. Mrs. Cluff, who was standing distractedly in the kitchen, waiting for the kettle to boil so that she would at least have the comfort of a cup of tea, hurried to let them in.

"Which room is it?" the older of the two asked her.

She pointed from the second stair. "That one with the cup of tea outside."

She watched him try the door.

"It's locked on the inside," he announced, after putting his eye to the keyhole. "I'm afraid it means breaking it open. Unless we can get in through the window."

"I've looked," Mrs. Cluff told him, "and it's locked, and anyway I don't have a ladder."

"Then we'll have to break in."

He murmured something to his burlier companion, who put his shoulder against the side of the door and pushed. When nothing happened, he stood back and charged it with the same beefy shoulder. At the second impact, the lock yielded and with a sound of ripping wood the door burst open.

Mrs. Cluff remained standing on the second stair while the officers disappeared into the room. The older one emerged and spoke to her over the landing railings.

"I'm afraid he's dead all right. Would you mind just taking a look and confirming that he is your Mr. Fawzi?" When she hesitated, he said, "Apart from the fact he's dead, he's all right to look at. There's nothing messy about him."

Shepherded by the officer who put himself close behind her in case she should flake out, Mrs. Cluff stepped reluctantly into the room.

Mr. Fawzi lay in bed with only his head showing. His eyes were closed and his mouth sagged open with lips stretched back to reveal yellowing teeth. Though he was lying on his back, his head gave the impression of having fallen to one side. On the table beside his bed was a half-filled glass of water and a small brown phial bearing a chemist's label. The phial was empty and its cap lay on the table.

Mrs. Cluff nodded when the officer asked, "Is that Mr. Fawzi?"

He guided her out of the room and downstairs. "It looks a clear enough case of suicide," he said, "but I'm afraid your house is going to be turned into a bit of bedlam for the next hour or two. There are certain routine steps to be taken in a case of this sort, but we'll make as little nuisance of ourselves as possible. Though actually the matter will be out of my hands once I report back to the station. Anyway, why don't you make a cup of tea and stay here in the kitchen. While I go out to the car and send a message, I'll get P/C Franks to start taking a statement from you."

During the next couple of hours policemen came and went and

Mrs. Cluff remained in her kitchen drinking cup after cup of tea, in which from time to time she was joined by one or other of the officers. She answered innumerable questions and put her shaky signature to a statement, whose contents she had no recollection of immediately afterwards, even though she had given an abstracted nod when the officer read it over to her and asked if it was true. She'd likewise shaken her head when he'd asked her if she wished to alter it in any way. The only question which she herself had asked throughout the evening had been whether they would be removing the body before they finally left. On this she was reassured.

Mrs. Cluff had begun to wonder whether her house would ever be free of policemen, when there was a knock on the kitchen door and a tall, fair-haired man with slightly fleshly face entered, followed by a short, dark man.

"I'm Detective-Superintendent Kettleman and this is Detective-Inspector Evans." He glanced round. "May we sit down?"

Mrs. Cluff nodded. "Would you like a cup of tea? I think there's just enough in the pot."

"Speaking for myself, I could certainly do with a cup," Kettleman said heartily. In fact, it was the last thing he wanted at this moment, but there was nothing like tea for breaking the ice at police interviews.

"Please," Inspector Evans said when she looked at him.

Kettleman stirred his tea vigorously, and carefully drained the spoon of all drops before laying it in the saucer.

"I'm afraid you must be tired of answering questions, Mrs. Cluff, but there are a few I want to ask you myself, even though you may already have given the information to other officers. You may have gathered from the number of people who've been stampeding through your house these last few hours that Mr. Fawzi's death isn't all it seems to be at first sight."

From her expression it was clear that she didn't understand what he was driving at.

"It's not just a case of straightforward suicide," he went on. "We shan't know the actual cause of death until the pathologist has completed his post-mortem examination."

"You don't mean that he didn't kill himself?"

"He appears to have done so, but confirmation or otherwise must await the doctor's report."

"But if he didn't kill himself, what did happen?" she asked in a mystified tone.

"Put briefly, Mrs Cluff, the position is this. We have every reason to believe that your Mr. Fawzi was also known under the name of Gamel. And Mr. Gamel is someone we've been searching for over the past week in connection with another serious matter."

"Gamel?" she repeated the name as though trying to pinpoint a recollection. "Hasn't his name been in the papers?"

"That's right."

"I remember reading something about him when I was down at my sister's. I had no idea he was my Mr. Fawzi."

"Absolutely no reason why you should have had," Kettleman said, "though our enquiries this evening have put the matter beyond doubt." He paused. "So now you understand why we're particularly interested in his death."

"He was one of the best lodgers I've ever had. He was always very nicely spoken and he didn't have any dirty habits like some of them."

"How long had he been with you?"

"Only a month."

"What did you know about him?"

"He came from Egypt or the United Arab Republic as he always insisted on calling it. He was over here studying."

"Did he tell you what he was studying?"

"It was economics."

"I'd like to know something about his routine, Mrs. Cluff. What time did he come and go?"

"I used to knock on his door at eight o'clock and leave a cup of tea for him. And he'd come down to breakfast by half past and be gone just before nine o'clock."

"And what time used he to come back in the evenings?"

"He used to come in and have his tea about six o'clock and then very often he'd go out again. When he didn't, he'd go upstairs and read in his room. He was a great reader. Of course, he had all his studying to do, too."

"Did anyone ever visit him here?"

"No. I gained the impression that he didn't have many friends."

"Where used he to go when he went out in the evenings?"

"He always said he was going to classes. I didn't question him about where he went. After all, it wasn't any of my business."

"Quite. Did he ever mention names to you? Names of people he was meeting or going around with?"

Mrs. Cluff shook her head. "No, I don't remember any names. He was a quiet, reserved gentleman."

"Everything a lodger should be, in fact?" Kettleman remarked with a smile.

"Yes, as I've said. He'd sometimes tell me about a funny incident at his classes. Something someone had said or done, but otherwise he didn't talk very much."

"Did he ever tell you anything about his family?"

"Only that his father was dead and that his mother and a younger brother lived in Cairo. And he had a married sister who lived in Alexandria."

"Used he to receive letters from home?"

"He never received any letters while he was with me. Perhaps they used to go to the college he attended."

"Perhaps. Did you take up any references when he came to you?"

"References? Certainly not. He paid a week's board and lodging in advance and my instinct did the rest." She bit her lip. "Whatever's proved against him, I shall still say that he was a very nice gentleman."

"I'd like finally, Mrs. Cluff, to ask you a few questions about the day you went away. That was last Saturday week?" She nodded. "What hour did you leave the house?"

"About a quarter to eight. That's why I left Mr. Fawzi his cup of tea half an hour earlier than usual. I'd told him I wouldn't be seeing him in the morning when I said good-night to him the previous evening."

"And you left him a note as well?"

"Yes, just reminding him of the day I was coming home."

"Was it intended he would manage for himself while you were away?"

She nodded. "Of course if I hadn't completely trusted him, I'd have had to ask him to go elsewhere while I was away. Either that or to have stayed at home myself."

"Did you knock on his door that Saturday morning?"

"Yes. I called out that I was just off."

"But you didn't get any reply?"

"No."

"Did you try the door by any chance?"

"No."

"So you don't know whether it was then locked or not?"

"I can't say."

"What was the last time you saw Mr. Fawzi?"

"About seven o'clock on the Friday evening. He came in a bit later than usual and only picked at his tea. He seemed to be worried about something."

"Worried? In what way?"

"He seemed depressed and nervous."

"Did he give any indication what was on his mind?" Kettleman asked intently.

"No. It was obvious that he didn't want to talk at all, so I just served him his meal and he went up to his room immediately afterwards, having eaten scarcely anything."

"And that was the last time you saw him?"

"Yes."

"Did you hear him leave the house later in the evening?"

"No."

"You mean you didn't hear him?"

"I mean he didn't go out."

There was a tense silence before Kettleman said with slow emphasis, "I don't want there to be any misunderstanding over this, Mrs. Cluff. Are you saying that Mr. Gamel—let's call him by his correct name—came in sometime before seven o'clock that Friday evening and that he never went out again?"

"It's the truth."

"And would you stand in the witness-box and swear to it on oath?"

"Naturally, if it's the truth."

She didn't understand why the two officers exchanged such obvious significant looks.

13

On the mornings when her employer was going to court, Sheila Gillam endeavoured to arrive at the office a quarter of an hour earlier than usual in order to have his letters ready for his attention, neatly piled in order of apparent importance with envelopes slit.

Her husband was wont to grumble at her on these occasions, not caring to recognise that she was putting herself out for another male, albeit her employer. Masculine myopia also enabled him to overlook the fact that, but for his wife, they'd often be unable to pay the rent when it fell due.

On the morning of the hearing of the Berg case, she reached the office at a quarter to nine. As she hurried along the south side of the square, she looked for Richard's car. She didn't see it and safely assumed she'd arrived first. However, on reaching her room, she found him standing in the doorway between their offices, looking slightly cross and impatient.

"Oh, good morning, Mr. Monk," she said breathlessly, "I didn't see your car outside."

"It's in for a service. I came by tube."

"How'll you get to court?"

"Taxi—or ambulance."

"Ambulance! Are you ill?"

"Not ill, just bruised and sore. Why do working girls these days have to carry great baskets! It oughtn't to be allowed in public transport during the rush hours. I got caught between two and my hips were almost ground away."

Sheila smiled indulgently. "They're a fashion. They look much better than those air travel bags, which are so pretentious, anyway. All labelled Pan Am or Air France when you're certain their owners have never been closer to flying than travelling on the upper deck of a bus."

"I don't mind that. The point is they're much softer than those baskets. And honestly one of the girls looked just like a giant panda."

"Perhaps it was a panda."

"Wearing brown knitted pyjamas?"

"You certainly seem to have had strange travelling companions this morning, Mr. Monk."

"This one was strange, all right," he muttered darkly.

Sheila hung up her coat and changed her shoes. She couldn't help feeling that for thirty-one her employer was beginning to show middle-aged hardening of the arteries. It really was time he found a wife. Besides, that flat, that car and all that money were terribly wasted on just him.

She began to sort through the letters which she had brought upstairs with her. When she took them into Richard's room, he was standing in front of one of the windows, hands thrust deep into pockets and staring out like a Victorian paterfamilias. He turned and came over to his desk as she put down the neat stack of letters.

She hesitated a moment before saying, "Is anything wrong? I mean, you seem worried."

"It's this case."

"Something new happened?"

"The police have found Gamel, dead. It's not just that, but I feel sure thay have something up their sleeve. Superintendent Kettleman was curiously evasive when he telephoned me yesterday evening. Just stated the bare fact and added quickly—too quickly—that he couldn't say anything further for the moment. He murmured about enquiries still continuing into the man's death."

"When did they find him?"

"That's another thing! I gather several days ago, but Kettleman pretended he hadn't 'phoned me before as they weren't a hundred per cent certain about his identity."

"I haven't seen anything in the newspapers about it," Sheila said with a frown.

"The police have managed to keep it out. All that's appeared has been a small piece about the suicide of a Mr. Fawzi. And who was going to connect Fawzi with Gamel until the police wanted them to!"

"I suppose it was a case of suicide?" Sheila remarked.

Richard gave an exasperated shrug. "I'm left not knowing what to believe. And what riles me is I'm damned certain that's how Kettleman intended I should be left!"

"Well, you're bound to learn the truth at court this morning."

"I prefer to know the truth before I arrive in court," he said crossly. "Or certainly the truth about an issue as vital as this."

"If Gamel did commit suicide, doesn't it help Mr. Berg?"

"In what way?"

"It bears out that Gamel murdered Parsons. That was the reason for his committing suicide."

"Unfortunately, that's not the only possible explanation. I know that a number of murderers have subsequently committed suicide, but they've usually belonged in the crime passionelle category or with the utterly mad. And Parsons' murder certainly wasn't either of those."

"What do you think the truth is then?"

"I don't know. I just don't know. I only hope it won't be too blasting to Berg's defence when it does emerge." With sudden decision, he sat down and picked up the top envelope. "I'd better get on with this lot. Fetch your notebook, Sheila, and we'll start. Incidentally, go easy on making any lunch dates for me over the next week or two. I'm going to be pretty tied up on this case."

"By now your friends are used to that," she remarked with a smile.

On the days when he was due to appear in court, Alan Scarby didn't normally go into Chambers first. The only exception was when he had a case in the High Court itself.

He pushed his cup across the table for more coffee and Jane, who had the baby balanced on one knee, poured it out for him.

Alan looked at his daughter and winced.

"I must say that a half-chewed and well-slobbered-over rusk is a most revolting sight at breakfast." Sophie gave him a delighted splutter and jabbed the rusk in his direction. "To think that in sixteen years time or so, she'll be an absolute honeypot."

"You hope!"

"Well, don't you think she will be?"

Jane gave her daughter a dispassionate gaze. "Quite possibly," she said slowly "Though don't forget it's always father's job to keep the more aggressive bees at bay."

"I'll have my swat ready." He looked at his watch. "I've time to read the paper before I go. Unless," he added innocently, "there's anything you'd like me to do."

"You could wash up the breakfast things and make the beds and clean the bath and——"

"Oh, well, I'll read the paper then," he broke in with a grin.

Jane lifted Sophie and her rusk on to the other knee. "Will this case be finished today?"

"It should be. I shall be playing a largely listening role. Richard always likes me to ask a few questions so as the client thinks he's getting his money's-worth, but it's generally best to sit and listen to the prosecution's case. There's little one can do to knock it out at this stage unless the charge has been completely misconceived, and if one asks a lot of questions without a full knowledge of what's to follow one can do more harm than good."

"I never understand why Richard briefs you at the magistrates' court. Why doesn't he handle the cases there himself?"

"Probably because he wants to keep Sophie in rusks," Alan said lightly. In a more serious tone he went on, "For some reason, he just doesn't like advocacy. He never has. In the circumstances, it's curious that he has this passion for the criminal law. One might have expected him to have eschewed any work which took him near a court. But not so. What's more he's a first-class instructing solicitor; never misses a point. At the same time he's not constantly passing up illegible notes and tugging at one's gown when one is on one's feet. I can't tell you how irritating that can be!"

"I really must find him a wife before it's too late," Jane murmured distantly. "He needs looking after."

"Like a bag of steel nails, he does."

At this point the conversation was brought to an abrupt close by Sophie who managed to loop her rusk into his full cup and spatter the front of his shirt with coffee.

"Loathsome brat," he said to her equably, as he went off to change.

Patrick Femmer arrived at court alone. He had taken Beth Steen out the previous evening and had suggested that he should pick her up in the morning. However, she had not only rejected the offer, and somewhat brusquely at that, but had said that there was no real need for him to attend at all and that he could be better employed back at the office. He, in turn, had resisted the suggestion and pointed out that this was an occassion for a show of solidarity and loyalty toward their harassed employer. The very fact of their presence must bolster Mr. Berg's morale, he had argued. It was very important that he shouldn't derive any impression of having been deserted by his staff.

Beth Steen had wanted to say that so long as she was there, there was no possibility of his feeling deserted, but had not been able to bring herself to voice this view. The result had been a slight constraint between them at the end of an agreeable evening.

Nevertheless, Patrick Femmer felt cheerful as he approached court the next morning.

"Excuse me, but don't you work for Mr. Berg?" Femmer had just turned into the court building and found himself confronted by a small, rather fat man with an undisguisably shifty smile. "My name's Berry. I'm on the *Gazette*."

Femmer looked at him gravely.

"You're not being called by the prosecution, are you?"

"No, I've just come to support Mr. Berg by my presence."

"There's no reason why we can't talk freely then. One always has to be a bit careful with witnesses, that's why I asked first. Police like to think they have a proprietary interest in anyone giving evidence for the prosecution. What they'd really like to do is hold them all incomunicado until the whole trial is over and done with. But since that's not possible, they hang warning notices round their necks, saying, 'Police Witness. Keep Away.' I'm speaking metaphorically, of course." He grinned conspiratorially. "But what I was wondering, Mr. Femmer—by the way it is Mr. Femmer, isn't it?—was whether you or anyone else in Mr. Berg's firm had any idea what he was up to? I mean, were you aware of his spying activities?"

"We don't even know now what he's supposed to have done," Femmer said cautiously.

"Don't you think his secretary, Miss Steen, must have had an inkling?"

"Hadn't you better ask her that yourself?"

"I very likely shall. How long is it she's worked for Mr. Berg?"

"About five years, I believe."

"But at any rate you had no idea what was going on?"

"Absolutely none."

"Must have come as a terrific shock?"

"It most certainly did."

"I'm trying to piece together the bits for an article which'll come out when the case is all over. Assuming he's convicted, of course."

"Do you think he will be found guilty?" Femmer asked anxiously.

"If all I hear is true, he's as good as sentenced now, except where there's a jury there's always hope." He laughed at his quip and Femmer gave him a look of worried enquiry.

"What is it you've heard?"

"That this Gamel story is going to blow up in his face. That was a gamble which hasn't come off, if you'll forgive the pun." Observing Femmer's blank expression, he added, "Gamel, gamble." His gaze, which had never stopped revolving like a lighthouse beam while he had been talking, now became focused on the door. "Ah, here's Mr. Monk arriving. I must go and have a word with him."

He departed abruptly from Femmer's side and trotted off to intercept Richard before he could disappear into the jailer's office.

"Remember our conversation last week, Mr. Monk?" he said with a sinewy smile.

"Which conversation are you referring to?" Richard enquired coldly.

"When I told you and Mr. Scarby that it only needed something else to happen on a Friday."

"And has it?"

"You should know."

"Well, I don't."

"What about Gamel's death?"

"What about it?"

"Didn't that take place on a Friday?"

"Are you telling me or asking me?"

"Well, isn't it what you've heard?"

"I've heard nothing except that Mr. Gamel has been found dead."

"I believe that the police have proof that he died on the same Friday as Parsons."

"Oh!" Richard tried to sound casual. "That still doesn't mean he couldn't have committed the murder."

Berry gave him a quizzical sidelong glance and Richard went on hastily, "What I do remember from our last conversation was your expressing the firm view that Gamel had got out of the country."

"I reckoned he'd either flown or would be found dead."

"I don't recall your saying anything about the possibility of his being found dead."

Berry shrugged as though it was a point of little importance. "Anyway, how's it going to affect Berg's defence?"

"How can I tell until we know what the evidence is!"

The newspaperman, who had been intently scanning the faces of further arrivals, now said in a distant tone, "We must have another chat later on, Mr. Monk. You never know, the *Gazette* might be able to help your client in some way." He gave Richard a tired flip of the hand and sidled over to a group of colleagues outside the entrance to the court. Richard made his way to the now familiar cell in which Berg was sitting, nervous and tense.

"What's this about Gamel being found dead, Mr. Monk?" he asked, jumping to his feet as soon as Richard entered. "There were just a few lines in the paper I saw in Brixton."

"It's apparently true," Richard said in a carefully judicial tone, "though I don't know much more myself. Superintendent Kettleman wasn't forthcoming when he telephoned me the news. However, we'll find out the truth soon enough this morning, so don't let's embark on speculation now."

Berg bit his lip and frowned as unspoken thoughts crowded through his head.

"If it wasn't Gamel who 'phoned you the other night, who could it have been?" he asked.

This was a question which had also been gnawing at Richard's mind, but he replied briskly, "I've just said, there's no point in speculating. Now when we get into court, I'll give you some paper and a pencil and I want you to note down anything which occurs to you as you listen to the prosecution evidence." Berg nodded like an obedient pupil and Richard went on, "I always remind my clients that the whole object of the preliminary hearing—which is today's stage—is to inform the defence of the case they have to meet. In due course we shall receive copies of the depositions, but there are likely to be a number of points which crop up and which won't necessarily be reflected in the witnesses' depositions. So it's really important that you listen to everything as intently as Mr. Scarby and myself."

"Has Mr. Scarby arrived yet?" Berg asked.

"I haven't seen him this morning, but you needn't worry, he'll be here all right. I've seen Mr. Femmer outside and I gather Miss Steen's coming."

Berg's attention appeared to wander. Then looking straight at Richard with a small rueful smile catching the corners of his mouth he said, "It's extraordinary what prison does for one's outlook. Previously important things seem suddenly trivial. Only one thing matters. Survival. Didn't somebody once say that there was nothing like the prospect of being hanged to help concentrate the mind?"

"Dr. Johnson, I think it was."

"He was right, too. And for this purpose, there isn't all that much difference between life imprisonment and hanging." An infinitely wistful expression filled his eyes. "I've made myself face up to the prospect of something which a few weeks ago I'd have considered so grotesque as to be unimaginable. That I, Joseph Berg, stand the chance of being sent to prison for life for a crime I didn't commit."

"You're being morbid," Richard said awkwardly.

"Morbid? Or realistic? Do you know, Mr. Monk, that my wife and my home up in Hendon seem to belong to another incarnation? Even my business interests don't seem rooted in actuality any more. Personal survival is all that occupies my mind. Survival as a personality as opposed to a vegetable."

"Look here, Mr. Berg," Richard broke in firmly, "just listen to me. I'm sure you've heard often enough what an important factor morale and outlook are in a patient facing a serious operation. Well, they're no less important in someone standing trial —particularly an innocent person. So try to curb all this introspection; it can only erode your morale."

Richard was thoughtful as he left Berg and made his way towards the courtroom. Although Berg talked about innocence, his words could almost be said to have been belied by the sense of heavy fatalism which surrounded them. Richard found Alan talking to Paul Prentice, the representative of the Director of Public Prosecutions, who they both knew of old.

"Hello, Paul," Richard greeted him. "Whenever I see you, I always know the Director realises he's on a sticky wicket."

"Phooey to that!" Paul said cheerfully. "I only get sent out on the dead certs."

"Dead cert from whose point of view?"

"Law and order's, of course."

The door behind the magistrate's high-back leather chair opened and the court usher came bustling through. Mr. Chaplin was so close on his heels that he had taken his seat before the usher could call for silence. A second later Mr. Chaplin set the machine in motion with one of his brisk little nods in Prentice's direction. It was, however, Alan Scarby who rose to his feet.

"I have an application to make to you, sir. It is that you should hear these proceedings in camera. I don't need to remind you of your powers to do so and will concentrate only on the reason for the application. This case has already excited a good deal of publicity and an even greater amount of subtly disguised speculation about its background. If these proceedings today are fully reported in the national Press, as they are certain to be, it is quite certain that the jury which is ultimately empanelled to try Mr. Berg must approach their task with preconceived ideas about the case. That is not only undesirable, but, much worse, it would be prejudicial to my client. I don't think I need say more than that, sir."

As Alan sat down, Richard glanced across at the table where a dozen newspapermen were sitting. A few of them looked glum, but most, frankly hostile. Berry caught his eye and made a grimace which seemed to say, "Trust you to cast a spanner in the works."

Mr. Chaplin looked enquiringly at Prentice.

"The prosecution is neutral in this matter, sir. I neither oppose nor support the application."

"In my opinion, Mr. Scarby," the magistrate said in brisk, astringent tones, "the desirability of a court functioning in public is paramount and I'm not satisfied that this is outweighed by any alleged prejudice which your client may suffer. I am satisfied that the normal safeguards are sufficient to protect his interests and I accordingly do not accede to your application."

Berry once more caught Richard's eye and gave him a triumphant leer.

Paul Prentice rose to his feet, propped a notebook against the ledge in front of him and began his opening speech. He was a man of around fifty with a relaxed air which belied a capacity for thoroughness, not to mention a tenacious competence. He had been in the D.P.P.'s office for twenty years and had come to view life with sardonic detachment. He had a wife, who wrote torrid romances, and four children, and he loved them all, as well as his dog and his garden. Family life was his safety valve.

He addressed Mr. Chaplin in an almost conversational tone.

"Shortly before ten o'clock on Friday evening the 4th of March, Frederick Parsons, a government servant in the Ministry of Defence, was murdered outside the Duchess of Bedford public house in Starforth Street. He was murdered by having a sharp pointed instrument plunged into his neck. He died within a matter of minutes. His assailant ran off along Starforth Street and was seen, shortly before he disappeared round a corner, by a group of people who happened to emerge from the Duchess of Bedford at that moment. They shouted to him to stop, but, perhaps not surprisingly, he continued to run away." Prentice turned a page of his notebook and flicked a glance toward Berg sitting in the small railed dock. "In the dead man's pocket," he went on in the same even tone, "was found a diary. And in that diary opposite the date of Friday the 4th of March appeared the name 'Berg', the name of the Duchess of Bedford public house and a time, ten o'clock. Mr. Berg was traced and was interviewed by Detective-Inspector Evans the next day. He was asked where he had been the previous evening and he said he had met a business friend, a Mr. David Reece, in the Queen's Head public house off Maddox Street in Mayfair and been in his company between nine and half past ten. Mr. Reece, however," Prentice went on in a tone as dry as quinine, "says that he never met the defendant that Friday evening, and moreover enquiries further show, in so far as such a negative can be proved, that the defendant was not at the Queen's Head public house when he says he was. And if he didn't meet Mr. Reece and he wasn't in Mayfair, what was he doing around ten o'clock that evening? And why did he see fit to lie to the police about his movements? In the submission of the prosecution, both those questions are answered in one. It was he who murdered Parsons." He turned another page of his notebook, took a sip of water, and once more faced Mr. Chaplin's

103

unwavering gaze. "I have mentioned, sir, the entry found in the dead man's diary and I shall be calling evidence before you that the defendant and the deceased had known each other for several years and, indeed, lived within half a mile of one another in Hendon."

Prentice drew a deep breath and squared his shoulders for the pronouncement which he knew everyone was waiting to hear. The indication of the motive for an otherwise motiveless crime. The trouble was that it was a motive on which the prosecution had felt obliged to hang its whole case. If it had been possible to avoid suggesting a motive, they would much prefer to have done so, but without pointing to a strong motive the Crown case was relatively thin. The motive was what bound the other elements together. On the other hand, it was a motive of such hidden and unknown implications that to introduce it in evidence was rather like running the risk of starting a bush fire in order to boil a kettle at a picnic. Discussion of the matter had occupied many hours in the D.P.P.'s office during the past five days. Eventually it had been decided that the particular nettle—it was seen as nothing less—would have to be grasped and the best hoped for.

"Although, sir, as you are well aware, it is not incumbent upon the prosecution to prove a motive, in this case they propose to do so, since the motive in question provides the strongest piece of evidence of all against the defendant. Indeed it provides that conclusive link between him and the dead man, Parsons."

The newspapermen sat with pencils expectantly poised. Beth Steen's brow was creased in a forbidding frown. And Detective-Inspector Pullar stood against the wall behind the witness-box with arms folded across his chest and an expression of superior boredom on his face.

"It is not, however, without the most careful consideration that the prosecution has decided to introduce this question of a motive, and it does so with a full sense of responsibility of the inevitable repercussions which will ensue. As I mentioned at the outset, Frederick Parsons was employed in the Ministry of Defence. His work there gave him access to certain classified material in the field of weapon research and development, and"—here prosecuting counsel's voice became suitably grave—"it is now unhappily beyond dispute that he abused the trust placed in him and passed government secrets to those not authorised to receive them. In

particular he passed them to the defendant on a number of separate occasions and the defendant, by inference, passed them to a
foreign power."

Alan rose to his feet. "I hope I may be forgiven for interrupting
my learned friend, but I would ask you, sir, to require him either
to explain or to withdraw the expression 'by inference'. It has a
most prejudicial ring about it and should not, in my submission,
be left hanging in the air."

"Well, Mr. Prentice?" the magistrate enquired crisply.

Prentice licked a small bead of sweat from his upper lip.

"What I meant, sir, was that the prosecution will call evidence
from which the permissible inference will be that the defendant
was passing material to a foreign power. Material which he had
received from Parsons."

"Is that all my learned friend is going to say on the subject?"
Alan asked in a voice of forensic outrage.

"I see no need to say more at this stage, sir," Prentice replied.

Alan looked hopefully at Mr. Chaplin who said, "I have no
power to compel the prosecution to say more than they want."

Prentice continued, "Finally, sir, before I call the evidence
before you, there are just two other matters I should mention.
On the sole of the defendant's right-hand shoe was found a small
spot of human blood of Group O. The dead man's blood was
Group O. The defendant's own blood is Group AB. And the
other point is this. The murder weapon has never been found,
but a paper-knife which is in the shape of a stiletto is missing
from the defendant's desk drawer, having disappeared about
the time of the murder."

Prentice sat down, only to bob up again immediately and call
his first witness who was a police plan drawer.

Alan turned to Richard and whispered in a puzzled tone,
"What's their evidence about the paper-knife?"

"They can't possibly prove that it disappeared immediately
before the murder. In which event it's pure prejudice."

"Have a word with Berg." Richard slid out of his seat and
went across to the dock. He motioned Berg to lean forward so
that they could speak without being overheard.

"When was the last occasion you actually saw the paper-knife?"
he asked.

"I imagine I used it on the Friday morning, though I don't

105

actually recall doing so. I used it automatically if I had any letters to open. Surely there's no reason why I should remember one specific occasion."

Richard ignored the note of protest and said, "Mr. Scarby's wondering what witnesses they can call to testify to its disappearance."

Berg looked bothered, but could only shake his head. Richard became aware that Miss Steen was trying to attract his attention and he tiptoed across to where she was sitting, aware that Superintendent Kettleman's keen eye was on him.

"I think we'd probably better go outside," he said, as she began to whisper in his ear with the intensity of compressed steam.

They stepped out into the almost deserted vestibule.

"Have you any idea who else the police are going to call regarding the disappearance of the paper-knife?" he asked before she could go off on a tack of her own.

"There is only Miss Parrot." Her tone was a mixture of indignation and malice.

"Miss Parrot?"

"You remember, Mr. Femmer's ex-secretary. The one who drew the attention of the police to the fact that it was missing."

"You said ex-secretary."

"He gave her the sack the next day. She hadn't been at all satisfactory and that was the last straw. He told her in no uncertain terms that she had spoken out of turn and shown herself disloyal to Mr. Berg."

"I see." Richard was thoughtful. "I follow that she can give evidence about the paper-knife not being in its usual place on the day the search was made, though a police officer could do that equally well. What, at the moment, isn't clear to me is who proves when it was last seen." Beth Steen stared at him with lips parted in a fixed expression as though hanging on the oracle. With a touch of impatience, he went on, "Was Miss Parrot often in and out of Mr. Berg's office?"

"I didn't like her going in there at all."

This, Richard found easy to accept, though it didn't answer his question.

"But used she to do so?"

Beth Steen bit her lip. "She was an uppish girl. If I didn't happen to be in my office, she'd go straight into Mr. Berg. What's more I'm certain she used to wait until she knew I was out of my room."

"Hmm. Well, we'll just have to wait and hear what she says in the box. And now I must get back into court."

The plan drawer had been replaced by a photographer who was giving evidence of photographs he had taken at the scene of the crime and later at the mortuary. These were now bound in two separate albums, so that the more squeamish couldn't suddenly turn from one of "Starforth Street, facing south" to "view of dissected neck".

Alan glanced at him enquiringly as Richard resumed his seat.

"Only Femmer's ex-secretary. I'll explain during the adjournment." Alan nodded and returned his attention to the witness.

The next person to give evidence was Dr. Lancaster, the pathologist, who, as Prentice explained, was urgently required in another court and was therefore being called out of turn. His evidence was given with an air of clinical detachment so that one had the impression that he was just standing there while a tape played back what he had recorded in his office. His testimony was to the effect that Parsons had died as a result of a stab wound of the neck which had severed his jugular vein. A wound, he added, which was consistent with having been caused by a sharp, pointed instrument.

He faced Alan with an air of wary patience when he rose to cross-examine.

"Would you agree, Dr. Lancaster, that the wound you've described could have been caused by any one of a large number of sharp, pointed instruments?"

"I'm afraid I don't follow the import of your question."

"You don't need to follow its import in order to be able to answer it."

"I'm only a doctor. I can't answer what I don't understand."

Prentice grinned and Mr. Chaplin looked inscrutable. Alan decided to put on a long-suffering expression. "I'll try again," he murmured. "Are you suggesting, Dr. Lancaster, that the weapon which caused the fatal wound had any particular properties about it apart from being pointed and sharp?"

"I'm not."

"There was nothing unique about it, in fact?"

"I've never suggested otherwise."

"Can you say whether the wound was inflicted from behind or in front?"

The pathologist pursed his lips and glanced down at his notes.

"It was a typical back-hand blow," he said slowly, "and since its entry was on the right side of the neck, it must have been struck by a right-handed person who was facing the deceased at the time. The alternatives to that would be a left-handed person striking a back-hand blow from behind the deceased or a right-handed one striking a forehand blow from behind." As he spoke, he indicated with his own hands the various possibilities he was describing. "But in my view, having regard to the trajectory of the wound, the last two alternatives are much less probable than what I first said." He looked toward Mr. Chaplin. "There is a further point which I think I ought to add. Namely, this was an expert blow. By which I mean that it was struck by someone who knew how to use an instrument for that particular purpose."

"No evidence that our chap qualifies in that way, is there?" Alan hurriedly whispered to Richard, who shook his head. Alan turned back to the witness. "What makes you say that?"

"The cleanness of the wound and the apparently unerring aim with which it was struck."

There was no doubt that the pathologist's evidence left those who heard it in a thoughtful frame of mind, which lasted long after he had hurried off to the next court which awaited his presence.

He was succeeded in the witness-box by Mrs. Parsons, whose evidence, Prentice explained, was very short and whose protracted attendance he wished to avoid.

"How the prosecution love appearing all humanitarian!" Alan murmured to Richard.

The dead man's widow looked just as Richard remembered her when he and Berg had called the Monday evening after the murder and had a somewhat distressing interview. She put down the testament after taking the oath and blinked nervously behind her pair of outsize spectacles with their pale-blue frames. They were the only touch of colour about her, as she was dressed from head to foot in heavy black. Richard found himself unworthily wondering whether Kettleman had briefed her about what to wear.

Under Prentice's persuasive questioning, she told the court that although her husband had known Berg for several years, she'd never had any inkling of their meeting clandestinely until after his death.

"Would you look at this piece of paper please, Mrs. Parsons?" Prentice said, handing a heavily creased sheet of paper to the usher who bore it across to the witness.

Alan was immediately on guard, his senses alerted. He didn't know what was about to come, but he had to be ready to intervene.

"Have you seen that piece of paper before?"

"I have."

"When?"

"I was present when the police found it at the back of a locked drawer in my husband's desk a few days after his death."

"When you say the police, would that have been Detective-Inspector Pullar?"

"Yes."

"And whose writing is it on that piece of paper?"

"My husband's."

Alan rose to his feet.

"With respect, sir, this can't be admissible in evidence. A piece of paper bearing the dead man's writing cannot be admissible without proof that Mr. Berg was in some way a party to it."

Mr. Chaplin looked at prosecuting counsel. "Well, Mr. Prentice?"

"Perhaps I may be allowed to continue, sir," Prentice said gently, "when I think its admissibility and relevance will become apparent. If I may say so, I have been careful not to make the document a formal exhibit yet and my learned friend's intervention is premature." He turned his attention back to the witness.

"Is *all* the writing on that sheet of paper in your husband's hand, Mrs. Parsons?"

"No."

"Do you know whose writing the rest is?"

"They say it's Mr. Berg's."

"Really!" Alan exploded. "We can't have that. It's pure hearsay."

Prentice ignored him. "You don't recognise it yourself?" he enquired in the same tone of sweet reasonableness.

"No. I've never seen his writing."

Prentice addressed Mr. Chaplin. "I shall be calling evidence later on, sir, that some of the writing is in the defendant's hand." He glanced at Alan. "I'm sure my learned friend will accept that."

"I clearly can't sustain my objection if that's the position," Alan said stonily. "Perhaps we shall soon be allowed to know what does appear on this mysterious piece of paper."

"By all means. Mrs. Parsons, will you first read out what is written in your husband's hand?"

" 'Berg suggests contact on private office line, definitely not at home number,' " she read falteringly aloud.

"And above that, what is written in a different hand?"

" 'Liverpool Street 4267.' "

"You will hear, sir," Prentice said, once more addressing Mr. Chaplin, "that that is the telephone number of the direct line to the defendant's office." He turned back to the witness. "What appears on the other side of that piece of paper?"

"It's a receipted bill from a paper shop in Hendon."

"In whose name is it made out?"

"Mr. Berg's."

"And now perhaps the document might be formally admitted and given an exhibit number," Prentice said in a satisfied tone.

"I should like to see it," Alan said. The usher handed the piece of paper to him, and he and Richard bent their heads over it. "Better ask Berg if the telephone number is in his hand."

Richard nodded and went across to the dock.

"Yes, it's my writing," Berg said, his hand trembling as he held the document. "It was shortly after Parsons had approached me and he wanted to know how he could get in touch with me. He didn't have a piece of paper and I wrote down that number on the back of the paper bill which I happened to have in my pocket."

"Did Parsons write his bit in your presence?"

"I seem to remember his writing something, but I didn't see what."

Richard returned to his seat beside Alan and after a short, whispered colloquy, Alan stood up and said, "I reserve my cross-examination of this witness, sir."

The next three witnesses were customers of the Duchess of Bedford public house. Their evidence was more or less the same. They had left the pub together and had seen a man lying in the gutter on the opposite side of the street. At the same time they had become aware of someone running away from the scene up Starforth Street.

Prentice's final question to each of them was the same.

"Apart from the man running away up the street, did you see anyone else in the vicinity?"

"No," each replied in turn.

When it came to cross-examination, Alan asked them how long they had been in the public house that evening and what they had been drinking. He made no suggestion that their senses had been dulled through alcohol, but merely probed this aspect to find out whether such an attack might profitably be made at a subsequent stage. Though they admitted to a fairly heavy evening's drinking each was at pains to emphasise that he was none the worse for it at the end.

The only other matter which Alan brought out in cross-examination was that none of them was able to give any sort of description of the man whom they had seen running away.

They were followed into the witness-box by a trio, the effect of whose evidence was to disprove Berg's story to the police of having met a business friend in the Queen's Head off Maddox Street. Alan reserved his cross-examination in each case. On his current instructions, Berg was admitting that he lied to the police, and this at a later stage was going to have to be explained away as painlessly as possible. In the meantime, the only thing to do was to show an impassive front and deny Paul Prentice and the police officers any clue to the defence reaction to this evidence.

After this batch of witnesses came an official from the Ministry of Defence who was the man in charge of the section in which Parsons had worked. He wore a nervous, apprehensive expression and looked ready to scuttle away like a crab which finds the rock beneath which it has been sheltering suddenly removed. He testified that Parsons had had access to "secret" and "top secret" files, that he had not before his death come under suspicion, but that recent investigation had revealed certain irregularities in the handling of classified files which would have called for an explanation by Parsons had he still been alive.

His evidence was couched in the polysyllabic circumlocution behind which civil servants are apt to take refuge when finding themselves uncomfortably exposed. He might appear to be a sitting duck, but Alan realised that there were dangers in taking too many pot shots at him in cross-examination, personally tempting though this was.

"Are you saying, Mr. Blenkinsop," he enquired, "that your internal security was not all it should have been?"

"Of course, I'm not responsible for overall security. The rules are laid down by others. You'll appreciate that there is a great deal of classified material within my Ministry."

A silence followed. Eventually Mr. Chaplin looked at Alan.

"Yes, Mr. Scarby?"

"I was waiting for the witness to answer the question I'd asked him," Alan said sweetly.

"Then perhaps you had better ask it again."

"Certainly, sir. Mr. Blenkinsop, are you saying that Mr. Parsons was able to abuse his trust because of security weaknesses in your system?"

"I'm saying no such thing," Mr. Blenkinsop said, his voice rising to an indignant squeak. "Anyone can defeat any security system if they put their mind to it. Anyone I mean who has access to classified files in the course of their everyday work, as Mr. Parsons did. All I've said is that enquiries since Mr. Parsons' death have shown . . ."

"I don't want to know what the enquiries have shown," Alan broke in quickly, "it's hearsay evidence so far as this court is concerned."

Mr. Chaplin now turned his clinical gaze on the witness.

"I should like to get this clear in my own mind," he said. "Does what you've said amount to this; that Mr. Parsons was not under any suspicion before his death, but that subsequent enquiries have shown he would have fallen under suspicion had you known earlier what you now know?"

"Precisely, your Worship," Mr. Blenkinsop said, with a small bow of acknowledgement to one whom he felt he could regard with a sort of fraternal respect.

"Are you going to ask him if he knew about Parsons' previous conviction?" Richard hissed in Alan's ear.

"I think that's better left for the moment," Alan murmured.

"We can get it as a matter of record from one of the police officers, anyway."

Mr. Chaplin glanced at his watch. "I'll now adjourn till two o'clock."

As soon as the magistrate had disappeared through the door at the back of the bench, the court was filled with the chatter of released spirits.

"These seats are bloody hard," Alan remarked, as he massaged his backside.

"I hadn't noticed," Richard said in a vague tone as he watched Miss Steen and Femmer leaving together. He had observed the rather embarrassed smiles of encouragement they had given Berg as he was ushered out of court.

"Come off it, Richard, you're not that physically tough. These seats would make even an elephant wriggle." He glanced across to where prosecuting counsel was gathering up his papers and speaking to Kettleman. "Let's have a word with Paul before he disappears."

"Seems to be going along all right, don't you think?" Prentice said cheerfully, as they joined him.

"The case?"

"What else?"

"All right for whom?"

"I meant all right for everyone from the point of view of time."

"Oh, yes, no complaints on that score. We shall finish comfortably this afternoon, shan't we?"

"Certainly, unless you suddenly start cross-examining at length."

"Seems unlikely. There is one matter I'd like to ask you about, Paul."

"Go ahead."

"I notice you didn't make any reference to Gamel in your opening. Are you calling any evidence about his death?"

Prentice shook his head. "Why should I! It forms no part of the case for the prosecution." He smiled wryly, "I'm not even sure whether it forms part of your case. Mind you, I'm not asking; but, as far as I'm concerned, Gamel only becomes relevant if and when your client officially puts forward the defence that Gamel murdered Parsons."

"I see," Alan said in a thoughtful voice. "Don't answer this if you don't want: but what would be your evidence about Gamel if you did call it?"

"Speaking off the record, Alan, it would be to the effect that Gamel could not have murdered Parsons and that he died by his own hand."

"What was cause of death?"

"A massive overdose of amytal. He'd cashed a prescription for a new supply of sleeping tablets that day and consumed the lot in one."

"And as far as your evidence goes, it's quite certain he couldn't have killed Parsons?"

"Quite. His landlady is absolutely positive that he never left the house after coming in shortly before seven o'clock."

"Thanks for the help, Paul." He turned to Richard. "We'd better go and grab something to eat. It's nearly half past one already."

They walked to a pub a hundred yards from the court, and after fighting their way to and from the bar sat in a corner with a plate of ham sandwiches and two half pints of beer.

"Do you think I ought to cross-examine Inspector Pullar about Gamel, Richard?" Alan asked through a mouthful of food.

"Yes, but limited to eliciting the fact that he was an agent masquerading as a student."

"Will Pullar admit that?"

"I'm certain Special Branch know quite a bit about Gamel. Anyway, it's worth probing. But we don't want the evidence about his death coming out at this stage. At least, not the evidence that he couldn't have killed Parsons."

"I agree. It's just a matter of cross-examining far enough to lay a foundation for something further later on." Alan drained his mug and put it down. "If—and I repeat—if Gamel couldn't have murdered Parsons, it places Berg in an extremely precarious position. He's already a proven liar once. . . ."

"If he sticks to the Gamel story, they'll certainly call rebutting evidence," Richard observed gloomily. "And if he doesn't—"

"If he doesn't, he's had it," Alan said.

"In that case, we must rely on being able to crack the evidence that Gamel could not have killed Parsons."

"And if we can't, he's also had it." Alan stood up. "Time to get back to court, Richard. If we've achieved nothing else, we've managed to persuade ourselves that our chap hasn't much of a hope."

Richard's jaw set in a determined expression, but he said nothing and followed Alan outside into the street.

As they entered the court building, Miss Steen and Femmer, who had clearly been waiting for their return, approached.

"You can speak to them," Alan murmured hastily. "I want to read through my notes."

"How is the case going for Mr. Berg?" Femmer asked.

"It's too early to start making assessments," Richard said in a bedside voice.

"As long as there've been no surprises," Femmer remarked.

"I don't think there've been any of those," Richard replied in the same tone.

"Personally, I thought it all sounded awful," Beth Steen broke in. "That prosecutor and the witnesses all trying to give the impression that Mr. Berg couldn't be other than guilty."

"That's a far too subjective view, Beth," Femmer said.

"I can't help it. That's how it struck me. Incidentally, Mr. Monk, I saw Miss Parrot here talking to one of the police officers when I came out of court at lunchtime."

Five minutes later, as it turned out, Miss Parrot took the oath as the first witness of the afternoon session.

She was a short, slim blonde girl with an urchin haircut and a terrified expression. Her voice barely rose above a whisper in reply to Prentice's opening questions, and several times she had to be exhorted to speak up. In a kindly tone by Paul Prentice; in a more peremptory one by Mr. Chaplin, after Alan had complained in a voice choked with forensic exasperation that he could scarcely hear a word the witness was saying.

"Until a short time ago, Miss Parrot, were you employed as a secretary by the firm of Joseph Berg?" Prentice went on.

"Yes."

"Do you know the defendant, Mr. Berg?"

She threw Berg a timid look. "Yes."

"For whom did you work as secretary?"

"Mr. Femmer."

"Is he the business manager?"

"Yes."

"Did you ever have occasion to enter Mr. Berg's office?"

"Yes."

"When?"

"If Mr. Femmer asked me to fetch something from Mr. Berg." In a bolder tone she continued, "And if Mr. Berg's own secretary didn't happen to be in her room."

"That's Miss Steen?"

"Yes."

"Were you present in Mr. Berg's office when the police searched it after he had been arrested?"

"Yes."

"What date was that?"

"It was a Wednesday."

"And what did you notice in the course of that search?"

"That the paper-knife was missing from his desk drawer."

"Can you describe this paper-knife, Miss Parrot."

"It was shaped like a dagger. It had a sharp point and a handle."

"What sort of length?"

"About twelve inches, I'd say."

Leaning forward as if to give emphasis to his question, Prentice asked, "When was the last occasion you saw it?"

"The previous Friday morning."

"That is, the day of Mr. Parsons' death?"

Alan jumped to his feet. "If that's meant to be a question, it's clearly one which is beyond the witness' own knowledge to answer. If it's a comment, it's highly improper."

"She has said 'the previous Friday' and that sufficiently establishes the date," Mr. Chaplin observed. "There's no need to pursue the matter further."

"If you please, sir," Prentice said equably, acknowledging the judicial rebuff. "What were the circumstances, Miss Parrot, in which you saw the paper-knife on the Friday?"

"Mr. Femmer asked me to take some letters into Mr. Berg for his approval, and there was also one addressed to Mr. Berg which had come to Mr. Femmer by mistake. While Mr. Berg was reading through the letters, he took the paper-knife out of the drawer and slit open the envelope of the other one."

"You're quite sure about that?"

"Yes." The small, cool voice seemed to add to the potency of her reply. Prentice sat down with a satisfied expression.

Richard once more dodged back to have a snatched word with Berg. "Is that true what she says about the Friday morning?"

"I think it is, as far as I remember."

"You did use the paper-knife in her presence that morning?"

"I can't dispute it," he said helplessly. "But there must be an innocent explanation," he added in a worried tone. "It must have fallen down the back of the drawer or become mislaid in some other way. I'm certain it'll turn up."

Richard nodded but made no comment. He would ask Miss Steen to have the office searched from top to bottom. The prosecution were clearly making an issue out of its disappearance, and the defence must be ready to deal with it. He returned to his seat. Alan had meanwhile begun to cross-examine Miss Parrot.

"How long had you worked for Mr. Berg's firm?"

"About six months."

"Were you happy there?"

She gave a shrug. "It was all right in some ways."

"Do I gather that you didn't get on with everyone?"

"Not everyone."

"Did you get on with Mr. Berg?"

"I liked Mr. Berg all right."

"Mr. Femmer?"

She shrugged again but did not answer.

"Did you get on with Mr. Femmer?" Alan repeated.

"So, so."

"Miss Steen?"

"Miss Steen didn't like me," she said sharply.

"And you didn't like her?"

"I had no reason to."

"Why did you leave the firm?"

She bit her lip. "To better myself."

"Or was it because you were given the sack?"

"I'd have left anyway."

"Given the sack because you were a very unsatisfactory employee?"

"That's not true. I was given the sack because I wouldn't do what they said."

"Who said?"

"Mr. Femmer and Miss Steen."

"And what was it you wouldn't do, Miss Parrot?" Alan enquired, in a dangerously silky tone.

"They said I shouldn't let Mr. Berg down and that the paper-knife was irrelevant as he couldn't have murdered the man anyway."

"But you didn't agree with them?" Alan said, tauntingly.

"I've told the truth," she retorted.

"You've no idea what happened to the paper-knife after you left Mr. Berg's office on that Friday morning, have you, Miss Parrot?"

"No."

"As far as you're concerned, anything could have happened to it?"

"Yes."

"Thank you." Alan resumed his seat, also contriving to appear satisfied.

Miss Parrot clicked her way to the rear of the court where she sat down and studiously avoided looking in the direction of Femmer and Miss Steen, who were only a few places from her.

Prentice now began to call the police evidence, and Detective-Inspector Pullar was first into the witness-box.

It occurred to Richard as he listened that the Special Branch man said precious little in effect, but a considerable amount by inference. It seemed clear that the prosecution were trying to prove the motive, which they were asserting, by innuendo and by a few brush strokes round the edges of the canvas. It seemed as though the police might still be trying to piece together this aspect of the case and that their enquiries had some way to go. Richard wondered whether they even knew now Berg had been disposing of the information he received from Parsons. It became increasingly clear that it was going to be a major point of decision whether Berg would be well advised to make a complete confession, before his trial, of his part in the spying activities. If this was to be done, it would be a question of asking Pullar to go and see him in Brixton, or better still for Richard to forward to the Special Branch officer a full signed statement. The other matter which occurred to Richard was the growing necessity of obtaining evidence from Israel that Berg was not only not a mercenary, but that the information he passed was relatively unimportant.

He had still had no reply from the brother in Safad despite

having written a second time, and despite having also sent an urgent cable. If allegations of spying were going to be thrown around, however, it would be of great importance to show that this was spying in a very minor key and far removed from the normal run of such cases. And this, unhappily, could only be proved with the assistance of Berg's brother, who was being elusive. Though Richard hoped not deliberately so.

He brought his mind sharply back to what was going on in court as Alan rose to cross-examine Inspector Pullar, who was gazing about him with a Canute-like air. He was not a comfortable witness, and clearly didn't trust the lawyers on either side not to try and push him into revelations of matters which belonged in one of his secret filing cabinets.

"I want to ask you some questions about a man named Gamel," Alan said pleasantly. "You know whom I'm referring to?"

"I do." The tone was loaded with caution.

"Is it a fact that Gamel died a short time ago?"

"I have no personal knowledge of his death."

"Perhaps not," Alan remarked patiently, "but surely you're not disputing the fact?"

"No, but I should point out that I have only hearsay knowledge of it," Inspector Pullar replied in a tone of the utmost condescension.

Richard was always sardonically amused when police officers self-righteously prayed in aid the hearsay rule to avoid answering unpalatable questions. So often it was the other way about and they were trying to slip in bits of hearsay without being pounced on.

"I have no doubt that I shall be able to prove his death another way if necessary," Alan continued unperturbed, "but as it happens I'm not concerned with his death, only with his life. What nationality was he?"

"I'm not sure we've established that we're talking about the same man. . ."

"I'm quite sure we are, Inspector, so perhaps you'd answer my question?"

Mr. Chaplin turned a cold sea-green gaze on to the witness who said quickly, "He was an Egyptian."

"How long had he been in this country?"

"Two and a bit years."

119

"Doing what?"

"To the best of my knowledge he was an economics student."

"Did he do anything else apart from studying?"

"I'm afraid I don't follow your meaning."

"Well, let me put it this way. How does it come about that you know of him?"

"It was my job to do so."

"Shall we stop beating about the bush!" Alan said with an edge to his tone. "Is it to your knowledge, Inspector, that Gamel was engaged in spying activities?"

The Special Branch man looked appealingly at Mr. Chaplin who stared stonily to his front. Prentice, however, came to his rescue, and rising slowly to his feet said, "These are rather sensitive matters my learned friend is asking about. I don't know how far he intends to go, but it may become necessary—if you consider his questions to be relevant—to ask you to hear this part of the evidence in camera."

"I shall be reluctant to adopt that course," Mr. Chaplin remarked, "for the same reason that I rejected Mr. Scarby's application for the whole case to be heard in private, though the considerations are, in fact, quite different." He focused his gaze on Alan. "Can you give me some idea, Mr. Scarby, first to the relevance of your questions and secondly, if I'm satisfied that they are relevant, the extent to which you wish to develop this line?"

"I appreciate, sir, that Gamel is a new name in these proceedings," Alan said with the air of one eager to be helpful, "but it is a name which will figure prominently at the trial. I will even say, sir, that the part this man Gamel played in this whole affair will be of vital significance to the jury when they come to consider my client's defence, which, I'll say straightaway now, is a complete denial of the charge."

"Hmm!" Mr. Chaplin observed in a tone without scepticism. "Supposing I accept your questions as being relevant—or perhaps I should say, not so irrelevant that I ought to disallow the evidence—how deeply are you going to pursue the matter?"

"Not deeply, sir," Alan replied, after a quick, whispered word with Richard.

"Very well, let's see where that takes us," Mr. Chaplin replied, picking up his pen.

Alan addressed himself once more to the witness. "Let me

rephrase my last question in a manner which may make it easier for you to answer. In addition to studying economics, did Gamel have activities which brought him to the notice of Special Branch?"

"Yes," Inspector Pullar replied curtly. He had obviously hoped that the magistrate would shut Alan up altogether, and had no intention of submitting with good grace to his further questions.

"Have your recent enquiries shown that Gamel and Parsons knew each other?"

"Yes."

"And met from time to time?"

"It seems possible."

Alan looked thoughtful for a few seconds before bending down to have a further word with Richard. Then he said, "I have nothing more to ask this witness at this stage."

Inspector Pullar contrived to look like a Canute who had after all managed to hold the waves back.

Kettleman was the next witness. His was the relaxed and confident bearing of one who has stood in the witness-box more times than he cared to remember, and who could be neither daunted nor ruffled by anything anyone asked him. Not even difficult magistrates could put him out of countenance, and he had certainly never regarded Mr. Chaplin as belonging in that category.

Alan confined his cross-examination to eliciting that Berg was a man of unblemished character and of high repute with all who knew him, socially as well as in business. Kettleman readily conceded this.

After him came Detective-Inspector Evans, whose much more intense personality was reflected in the almost vocational fervour with which he gave his evidence.

Richard and Alan listened with carefully impassive expressions as he testified to the damning first interview with Berg. And damning he really made it sound.

"I think I'll reserve cross-examination," Alan whispered. "Do you agree?"

"We haven't yet elicited evidence of Parsons' previous conviction," Richard reminded him.

"What do you think?" Alan asked doubtfully.

"Since it's not going to affect the issue of a prima facie case, I'd be inclined to leave it."

"I think you're right."

"There's nothing else to ask him about at this stage," Richard observed. "Listening to Evans has merely served to sharpen the horns of Berg's dilemma."

"I know," Alan said, making a face.

Inspector Evans looked quite crestfallen when Alan announced that he had no questions to put to him. Confident of his answers, he had obviously looked forward to being cross-examined, but instead was made to feel like a circus horse denied the opportunity of performing its most carefully rehearsed trick.

It was about four o'clock, and the small fumed oak court-room had become intolerably stuffy, when Mr. Chaplin wrinkled his nose in distaste and said, "How much longer are you going to be, Mr. Prentice?"

"I have only one more witness to call, sir, and his evidence is extremely short."

This turned out to be Mr. Shove of the Metropolitan Police Laboratory whose evidence-in-chief lasted only ten minutes. He referred to his negative examination of all Berg's clothing, except for the right shoe which bore a spot of Group O blood on the instep.

"And what group," Prentice asked, "was the sample of blood taken from the deceased?"

"Group O."

"And that taken from the defendant?"

"Group AB."

"Thank you, Mr. Shove," Prentice said, and sat down with a sigh of relief.

Alan rose slowly at the same time reading the note he just taken of the witness's evidence.

"You have said, Mr. Shove, that you found no bloodstains on the defendant's jacket, trousers or shirt?"

"That is correct."

"Was there any evidence of their having been recently washed or cleaned?"

"No, none," Mr. Shove replied, after glancing down at his own notes.

"When I say recently, I mean within the preceding three days?"

"No, no evidence of that at all."

"Thank you. Now I want to turn to another point. Group O is a very common group, is it not?"

"The most common. Forty-seven per cent of the population have blood of Group O."

"So it would be well within the bounds of possibility for someone to pick up blood of that group accidentally on his shoe?"

"Mr. Shove is a scientific expert, not an actuary, Mr. Scarby," Mr. Chaplin said in a brisk tone. "Moreover, the point you're trying to make is one for a jury and not for me as an examining magistrate."

Alan smiled. Some magistrates let you get away with certain things and not others, and all a defending advocate could do was to probe until he met resistance. As Mr. Chaplin's observations were unanswerable, Alan felt obliged to accept defeat and move on.

"Tell me, Mr. Shove, would you have expected the person who stabbed Parsons to have got blood on his clothing?"

"Not necessarily."

"Surely it would have been more likely than otherwise?"

Mr. Shove assumed an expression of great thoughtfulness. When he spoke, he did so in a slow, ruminating tone. "I think I can only say that I wouldn't have been surprised to find blood on the killer's clothing; but equally I wouldn't be surprised not to find any." He gave Alan a helpless smile. "I'm sorry I can't be of more assistance, but so much would depend on factors not within my knowledge."

"Such as?"

"How close together the two men were. How the knife was withdrawn. Things of that sort."

"You know that the weapon has never been found?"

"So I understand."

"Assume that the killer carried it away with him, would you not then have expected to find traces of blood on his clothing?"

"If he'd put it in his pocket or held it under his jacket, certainly I'd have expected to."

"But there were no such traces on Mr. Berg's clothing?"

"None."

"Did you examine the clothing of . . . of . . ."—Alan flicked back the pages of his notebook—"of Mr. Oakes, Mr. Parry or Mr. Sorrell? They were the three gentlemen who were first on the scene of the crime."

"No, I didn't."

"If you had done so, would you have expected to find traces of Group O blood on their shoes?"

Mr. Shove flashed him an amused smile. "Yes, I should, assuming that they went right up to where the dead man was lying."

Alan resumed his seat and Richard whispered, "A draw in our favour, at least."

Prentice announced that that was the case for the prosecution, and Alan informed the magistrate that his client pleaded not guilty and reserved his defence and didn't wish to give evidence or call any witnesses at that stage. After which Mr. Chaplin, with the minimum number of words, committed Berg for trial at the Old Bailey.

The small court-room emptied rapidly and there was left only the atmosphere of morning-after-the-night-before, less the smell of stale tobacco. All drama is ephemeral whether enacted in a theatre or in a court-room.

Richard and Alan quickly gathered their papers together and went out through the jailer's door to have a word with Berg before he was driven back to the prison. He looked drawn and confessed to having a splitting headache.

"I'm not surprised in that atmosphere," Alan remarked.

"I doubt whether the atmosphere had anything to do with it, Mr. Scarby," he said reproachfully.

"No, I know what you mean," Alan said in slight embarrassment. "I hope you weren't expecting any miracles at this stage?"

"You mean, I should reserve my expectations for later on?"

"I'm afraid I'm not expressing myself very well. I'm tired, too. What I meant was that today's proceedings went much as expected and that there was very little we could usefully do. But that doesn't mean we shall be inactive when it comes to the trial." Alan glanced around the small cell as though selecting his words off the walls. "Mr. Monk will be coming to see you in Brixton within the next few days, but what I should like you to be thinking about in the meantime is this. At your trial you'll be giving evidence and will, I have no doubt, tell the jury what you've told us. Namely, that you were a witness to Parsons' death but didn't kill him . . ."

"Gamel killed him," Berg said dully.

"In making that defence," Alan went on, as if the interruption had not occurred, "you will be obliged to admit that you lied to the police and it will be of vital importance for you to persuade the jury that even such reasonable people as themselves would have lied in similar circumstances. If you don't manage to do that, the outlook won't be very good."

Berg shook his head in weary despair. "I'm sorry I can't share your detachment, but perhaps that's more than even a lawyer would expect." With a spurt of vigour, he went on, "Look, Mr. Scarby, if I can't persuade you, my counsel, that I didn't murder Parsons, how can you persuade a jury?"

"It doesn't matter whether I believe you guilty or not," Alan replied irritably. "It does matter what view the jury take, and it's you in the witness-box, far more than anything I can say to them, which is going to be the decisive factor."

"I can only tell them that I did *not* murder Parsons," Berg repeated stonily. "And if they don't believe me, I shan't be the first innocent man to be wrongly convicted."

"Mr. Scarby is only trying to point out that your defence won't be entirely plain sailing," Richard broke in. "We've got to face the fact that if we allege Gamel was the murderer the prosecution will certainly seek to call rebutting evidence to prove that he couldn't have done it."

"But he did do it! He must have done it! There's some flaw in their rebutting evidence or whatever you call it. You've got to find out what it is, Mr. Monk. My whole life depends on it."

Alan said, "I'm sorry if I upset you just now, but I'm always anxious that my clients should realise how much depends on them and the impression they make in court. Believe me, I'll be doing my best, but I wouldn't want you to feel that my best is as important as yours in this particular case."

Berg looked up at him and said in a bleak tone, "From what you say, no one's best is going to save me if the prosecution manage to persuade the jury that Gamel couldn't have done it."

"I don't think this is the moment to start discussing details," Richard broke in quickly. "I shall be coming to see you in Brixton and we'll have an opportunity then of considering our whole plan of defence. There's a great deal of work to be done on it and we're not going to be idle these next few weeks."

As they made their way back through the deserted court-room, Alan said, "We'd better have an early con to discuss the case, Richard. I must say I can think of easier ones to defend."

"So can I. But I still don't believe he did it."

"Hmm! I wish you could be on the jury."

14

One evening about ten days later, Richard and Alan played squash. The game followed the now usual pattern, with Richard's stamina the decisive factor in his victory over the more accomplished player. After they had showered and changed, they went back to Richard's flat for a drink.

Alan glanced at the chair that resembled a sawn-off Scotch egg and backed into it. Richard handed him a long well-iced gin and tonic and sat down with a glass of Bulgarian white wine which he sipped meditatively.

"Any good?"

"Out of the ordinary."

"So is jet fuel."

"This has less of a kick."

"Oh, well, you can always use it for boiling eggs," Alan said with a grin. "I know all your cooking requires wine."

There was a silence while each felt luxuriously at rest after the hectic expenditure of energy.

"I went to see Berg again yesterday afternoon," Richard said.

"How is he?"

"He's still on about Gamel. *Insists* that it was he who murdered Parsons. Mind you, I can see it from Berg's point of view. Once he allows himself to be persuaded that Gamel didn't do it, he's a man without hope. The last glimmer has gone and he's a stranger alone in the dark."

"And nobody likes being alone in the dark."

"Exactly."

"But if Berg didn't murder Parsons and Gamel didn't, who did?"

"That, thank God, the defence don't have to prove."

"I know they don't, but if those are the only two horses in the race and the police can show conclusively that Gamel was not the murderer and we only have Berg *saying* that he didn't do it . . ."

"You mean the jury won't consider an unknown third possibility?"

"Why should they?"

For a minute or two each sat brooding in silence. Then Richard said, "I've still not had a word from Israel. I've sent two more cables, and even tried telephoning, but that was hopeless. I'm not even sure I was through to the right country."

"I wonder if we ought to try to enlist Pullar's assistance."

"I think it would be dangerous without knowing more about the background. We might only succeed in putting the police on to something highly damaging to Berg."

"There'd be that risk."

"After all we don't know anything about the people Berg was dealing with, apart from his brother. And we know precious little about him."

"And Berg doesn't know a thing about the others, he says."

"Quite. I imagine our security boys have their contacts in Israel, official and unofficial, but whether they're the same as Berg's or whether he was in touch with a completely different outfit, God alone knows. Certainly Berg himself doesn't know."

Alan tilted the remains of a lump of ice into his mouth and crunched it up as Richard winced.

"I think it's ominous that you've not heard from his brother. He's obviously received your cables, or I imagine you'd have been informed by the telegraph authorities. In which case, he must have decided to ignore your plea for help and let his brother be thrown to the wolves."

"In the best traditions of the Secret Service," Richard commented drily.

"On the other hand," Alan went on, "I agree with what you said at court the other day. Namely that if the prosecution are going to prove that spies falling out was the motive for this murder, it is very important for us to be able to show that Berg was not a real spy, but was merely somebody whose innocence and good nature and lack of guile led him to the touchline, one might say, but didn't make him one of the players. And the only way we can prove that—if we can prove it at all—is with the help of those he was in touch with in Israel."

"Another drink?" Richard asked, his eyes narrowed in concentrated thought.

Alan held out his glass and Richard crossed over to the drink cabinet in the corner of the room. There was a silence while he poured out the gin, cut a slice of lemon and added a couple of ice cubes and handed the glass back to Alan with a fresh bottle of tonic. The silence continued as he returned to the cabinet and poured himself out another glass of wine. After he had sat down again, he took a sip of his drink and said in a matter-of-fact tone: "There's only one solution. I shall have to go out to Israel myself." Observing Alan's quizzical expression, he added, "You see, I still think he's innocent."

15

Although Richard had travelled abroad fairly extensively, he had never been to Israel, nor, indeed, to any country in that part of the world. Mention of Israel, however, always brought to his mind a long sloping coastline with an intriguing carbuncle-like excrescence at the top end, since it had always given him particular pleasure tracing in this feature on the maps he'd drawn at school.

On the day after his decision to make the journey, he paid two visits. The first was to Brixton Prison to inform Berg and obtain his formal approval.

Berg appeared to be elated by his solicitor's enterprise, though he still clung to the hope that the absence of any response from Israel was due to mischance rather than blank refusal to come to his aid.

His excitement had suddenly evaporated, however, as he said to Richard, "Won't this cost an awful lot?"

"You needn't worry about that side of it," Richard had replied briskly. "Your defence won't cost you more than you can afford."

For a full minute, Berg had just stared at him.

"I don't know what to say, Mr. Monk," he'd murmured at last with a slight catch in his voice.

"Nothing to say. I only hope it'll prove a profitable trip."

"Of course, you'll cable my brother that you're coming?"

"Yes, I was proposing to do that."

"How long will you be away?"

"Three or four days. Five at the outside. I thought I'd stay in Haifa and drive to Safad from there. Do you agree that would be best?"

"Yes. In a private car, it will only take you a little more than an hour. And it's a very beautiful drive. You must make sure you go through Nazareth."

An hour later Richard was sitting in the tiny office of the travel agent to whom he'd been going for several years.

"I want to go to Israel, Mr. Brewster," he said as soon as the initial pleasantries were over.

"And when were you thinking of going, Mr. Monk?"

"Tomorrow or the day after."

It was because Mr. Brewster showed neither surprise nor agitation that he had so many steady clients bringing him their impossible demands year after year. His only reaction was to reach for the telephone.

"We'll get on to the airline first then."

Three minutes later he had reserved Richard a seat on a flight leaving the next morning, non-stop to Tel Aviv. "Actually the airport is at Lod, which is about twelve miles inland from Tel Aviv," he explained as he noted the flight particulars on a large pad of paper.

"I want to go to Haifa, as a matter of fact. Not Tel Aviv."

"Then you'll want a car to meet you and take you there," Mr. Brewster murmured, making a further note. "I'll cable our agent straightaway."

"Now for an hotel in Haifa." He glanced up enquiringly. "I take it you do want an hotel, Mr. Monk?"

"Please."

"Any choices?"

"As always, I leave it to you."

"Then you must stay at the Dan Carmel. It's a really elegant hotel and with one of the loveliest views you could ever wish for. Haifa Bay one side and open Mediterranean on the other."

"Sounds attractive."

"It is," he said enthusiastically, reaching again for the telephone.

One of the fascinating things about Mr. Brewster was that he always made it sound as if he'd only himself returned from that particular part of the world a few days before. There wasn't an hotel in seven continents about whose amenities he couldn't apparently discourse with recent personal reminiscence. And yet no one had ever known him not to be in his office.

Five minutes later, he said, "Well, that seems to be everything, Mr. Monk. I'll send your ticket and other documents round to your office this afternoon. I hope you have a very pleasant trip."

"Thank you, Mr. Brewster," Richard said, shaking him by the hand. "One day I shall see if I can really catch you out."

"In what way, Mr. Monk?"

"By saying I want to charter a camel across Japan."

"That might be a little difficult, I agree. Perhaps you'd accept a bicycle tour to Addis Ababa instead. I once had a client who set off on such a venture."

"How did he get on?"

"I've never heard. A nice man, though a trifle eccentric in some ways," Mr. Brewster mused.

The plane the next day was three quarters empty, and this coupled with a strong tail wind enabled it to cut half an hour off its scheduled time. Richard spent the journey reading the numerous pamphlets about Israel which Mr. Brewster had enclosed with his ticket. When he wasn't reading, he was eating and drinking and generally succumbing to the delightful feeling of euphoria which jet air travel induced in him. Though he always kept at the back of his mind the realisation that euphoria could without warning be translated into instant terror. On his various travels he had only once been really alarmed, and that was when the engine he'd been vaguely gazing out at began to belch smoke and flame. Half an hour later a planeload of very frightened passengers made a forced landing in Iceland and didn't even grumble when held up there for two days by bad weather.

On this occasion, however, there were no such alarms, and shortly before three o'clock he found himself stepping out of the plane into the warm breeze which was blowing across Lod Airport. One breath was enough to assure him that he had left behind the climate of Northern Europe.

It never occurred to Richard to doubt that Mr. Brewster's arrangements would be anything but perfect, even when made at such short notice, and so was ready for the man who approached him with a tentative smile as he emerged from Customs examination.

"Mr. Monk?"

"Yes."

"I'm Yuri. I'm driving you to Haifa. The car is outside. Please, I take your bag."

The car was a Vauxhall Victor, and Richard got into the front seat beside Yuri who at once began a running commentary which embraced everything within sight and lasted for the whole of the hour and a half drive to Haifa. Richard listened with one ear and murmured an appropriate observation from time to time, though his own attention was almost entirely focused on what he was seeing with his own eyes. Whenever he was in a new country he would observe his surroundings with fierce intensity and normally resent the distraction of a guide's patter. However, Yuri's unashamed eagerness to proclaim the virtues of his country and his obvious pride in its achievements had a charm which forestalled any irritation Richard might otherwise have felt.

It was a congenial landscape through which they drove, endless lush citrus and olive groves all laid out with geometrical neatness. And everywhere, as far as the eye could see in any direction, water sprinklers casting plumes of spray over the land. Richard commented on this.

"Water and hard work are our most vital assets," Yuri said enthusiastically. "There is no problem over hard work, but perhaps one day we must fight a war to make sure we have water."

"In England the problem is the other way about," Richard remarked, but Yuri only nodded absently.

"Every drop of water you are seeing, Mr. Monk," he went on, "comes from Lake Kinneret. What you call the Sea of Galilee. And Lake Kinneret receives its water from the mountains of Syria and Lebanon, and those countries are not friendly to us. They

131

would like to stop our water." His expression, which had become brooding, suddenly brightened as he continued, "Even in the desert, you will see water pipes everywhere, all from Lake Kinneret."

Richard's other main impression of the journey was of immensely virile looking young men and girls in army uniform standing at the four points of every cross-roads trying to thumb lifts. Not for them the turned back and weary thumb movement. They faced the oncoming driver and with an imperious gesture almost dared him not to stop. Yuri, however, didn't, and when Richard, uncomfortably aware of an empty back seat, suggested that they might offer a lift, he said that the car wasn't insured for that purpose and his company forbade. For the remainder of the journey Richard avoided meeting the gaze of these would-be passengers.

Yuri waved a hand in the direction of a line of brown hills a few miles to their east. "That is Jordan. Here, Israel is only twelve miles wide." With a chuckle he added, "The Arabs in Israel are more prosperous than the Arabs in Arab countries, so they hate us all the more. We do not hate them, but we must be prepared always to defend ourselves. To defend our water."

A few minutes later he asked, "How long will you stay in Haifa, Mr. Monk?"

"Three or four days, I expect."

"You want car for sightseeing?"

"I have to go to Safad tomorrow. Can you drive me there?"

"Sure I drive you. And we can see Nazareth and Tiberias, too. What time you wish to go?"

Richard frowned. "I can't say at the moment, I may have to see someone in Haifa first."

"You say time and I will be at hotel."

"Eleven o'clock then, but I may be late."

"I tell office you need the car all day. That is best."

"O.K. Do that."

There seemed no point in haggling about the extra expense this might involve. It wasn't likely to be very much, and it would certainly be convenient to have the car at his complete disposal.

"Here we come to Haifa," Yuri announced. "There is your hotel right on top of Mount Carmel."

Richard craned his neck to look and realised with an excited

tingle that it was situated on the carbuncle-like excrescence of his
school map days.

"Over there is Elijah's Cave," Yuri said, taking an easy leap
back through history. "It is very holy shrine, which you should
visit."

Richard tried to recall what he knew about Elijah, which was
not very much. In any event, he had not associated the prophet
with a hillside overlooking the Mediterranean. He thought he
could remember a picture, in a children's book of Bible stories he
had had, of a rather surprised and angry-looking old gentleman
soaring up into the air. "Elijah being taken up to heaven" had
been the caption.

"You see that golden dome?" Yuri asked, pointing at a prom-
inent edifice on the lower slope of Mount Carmel. "That is the
Baha'i Shrine."

Richard looked nonplussed.

"You have not heard of the Baha'i faith?"

"I'm afraid not."

"It is very good faith. Very peaceful. You must go there, too.
You will be interested."

Yuri was silent for the next five minutes as he negotiated the
steep, sharply bending road which led up to the hotel and to the
highest part of Haifa itself. Pleasant villas and apartment houses
were sprinkled over the hillside, and Richard thought how attractive they looked.

Nothing, however—not even Mr. Brewster—had fully prepared him for the superb view which greeted his eyes as he stepped
out on to his bedroom balcony. Haifa tumbled down the hillside
at his feet, levelling out as it neared the water. Beyond and to the
right the coastline made a great sweep northwards, and he could
see Acre fifteen miles distant and, beyond, the mountains which
marked the frontier with Lebanon.

For several minutes he stood and drank it in. Then a ship
hooted in the harbour below and he remembered that he had
work to do. There were several ships in port and he wondered
whether any of them belonged to the Shraga Shipping Company.

He had a shower, cleaned his teeth—which more than anything
else always made him feel ten degrees fresher—and put on
the only change of outer garb he had brought with him. This

133

included a saffron yellow knitted silk tie, which was the latest to have been added to his collection.

Before leaving his bedroom he studied a street plan and saw that Eilat Road, where the Shraga Shipping Company had its offices, was in the harbour district. Taking the plan out on to his balcony, he was able to identify the area in which the street lay without great difficulty.

It was with a confident and expectant step that he made his way to the underground station and journeyed down the mounain in what was a subterranean funicular. He emerged at the last station on the line to find himself at sea level, and in very different surroundings from those he had left behind at the top, which reminded him of middle-class Southern California. Here at the bottom the houses clung together in dilapidated clusters and the narrow streets were teeming with Arabs of all ages. Small ones whizzed between his legs, tall stately ones strode purposefully past, and bent old ones with nothing else to do stared at him with unashamed curiosity. His nose, too, was assailed by smells which certainly didn't belong to Southern California.

Richard was prepared to accept, as he'd been constantly told, that Arabs were extremely clean. All he knew was that a great number managed not to look it.

Eilat Road turned out to be little more than an alleyway, and he had to edge round a group of street vendors and their customers who all but blocked one end.

Under the intent scrutiny, he felt, of half of Haifa's population he walked slowly up the street searching for the Shraga Shipping Company office. Though he hadn't expected to find anything of the size of Cunard offices in London, he hadn't thought he'd be able to miss it, which was what he did manage to do.

Having reached the end of the street, he turned round to retrace his steps, aware this time of even greater interest in his presence.

It annoyed him that he felt uncomfortable under the impassive gaze of so many pairs of eyes, and he redoubled his efforts to appear unconcerned.

Once or twice he was jostled by the crowd and each time felt his heart miss a beat. Of course, it was absurd, since one could no more avoid being jostled in such a street, than one could on leaving Wembley after the Cup Final. He smiled to himself as he reflected that this was what came of reading too many thrillers. You were apt to see something sinister in every expression, once you were in unaccustomed surroundings. On the other hand he couldn't also help wishing he'd taken Karate lessons like so many of the heroes of his reading, if only in his case to surprise a common pickpocket who was after nothing other than his wallet.

He became suddenly aware of being under the particular scrutiny of a scrofulous-looking beggar sitting on a doorstep. He had a four-or five-day growth of grizzled beard and was dressed in Arab clothes so that a leathery face was all of him that was exposed. Though his other features gave the appearance of inexorable decay, his eyes were like two lumps of black onyx and looked anything but decayed. They fastened on to Richard and never left him. It was due to him, however, that Richard noticed the peeling sign which read "Shraga Shipping Company", repeated beneath in Hebrew. He had been so determined not to show any reaction to the Arab's disconcerting stare that he had stopped opposite him to take stock when the notice caught his attention.

It was on a door in front of which the man was squatting. Boldly Richard walked over to it and tried to see whether the company's hours of business were shown. The man made no attempt to move, but merely tilted back his head so that he was staring straight up into Richard's face. Richard leant over him and tried the handle, only to confirm that the door was in fact locked.

"Open soon?" he enquired, looking down at the man still squatting at his feet.

The man said nothing, but blew out his lips in what might have been anything from a small belch to a disdainful comment on Richard's presence.

Richard stepped back and looked up at the first-floor windows, though there was no indication whether these belonged to the shipping company or not. What did seem unlikely, from the outside appearance of the office, was that they could own anything more seaworthy than an old tramp steamer of first world war vintage.

He was still gazing up at the building when a voice at his side said, "Shalom. Shraga Shipping Company closed."

He turned to find a young man in European dress with a smooth, round face and a small, neat moustache.

"Closed! For good, do you mean?"

The young man shrugged. "Closed until it opens again," he said, with a faintly raised eyebrow as though he and Richard were fellow conspirators.

"How long has it been shut?" Richard asked, ignoring the suggestive eyebrow.

"One week? Not a big company, I think. Shalom."

And he walked away as suddenly as he'd appeared, and in no time was lost amongst the crowd.

Richard returned his attention to the doorway, which was now quite empty. The scrofulous Arab had disappeared as completely as the young man with the moustache.

Half an hour later he was back in his hotel. He went up to his room and strolled out on to the balcony. Far below him lay the harbour and Eilat Road. It all looked very peaceful and ordinary, which was certainly more than it had a short time before.

But looking back on his expedition now, he comforted himself by the reflection that it had revealed nothing which couldn't be explained in terms of normal occurrence.

He would try to find out something more about the Shraga Shipping Company before he left for Safad in the morning. Meanwhile, he proposed to do nothing more adventurous than have a good dinner and read the thriller he'd bought at Heathrow which, from its blurb, had the sort of hero to whom Richard's visit to Eliat Road would have been no more alarming than a lunchtime stroll in Bedford Square.

None the less, he was glad that he was going to have Yuri's company on the morrow.

16

It was on the next day that Beth Steen went to see Berg in Brixton Prison. After spending the morning in the office, she went home at lunchtime and changed into an emerald green suit with black trimmings which she knew he liked. In fact, she spent as long making herself attractive as if he'd been going to take her out to dinner at an expensive restaurant. And when she was ready to leave, she took a taxi so as to arrive, as near as possible, in the same freshly minted condition.

She'd been to see him at the prison once before and had found it a jarring experience. The crude lack of privacy and the awful institutional surroundings made it more of an ordeal than a pleasure, though she noticed that not everyone seemed to be similarly inhibited.

"Probably because they spend half their lives visiting menfolk in prison," she had reflected in silent disdain as she'd watched two particular women behaving as unconcernedly as if they'd been at the launderette.

She had been indignant to learn that lawyers were provided with better facilities when they came to interview their clients in prison and had commented querulously on the apparent discrimination against ordinary visitors.

"I imagine," Berg had said sardonically, "it's based on the expectation that visitors will try to slip us hacksaw blades and telescopic ladders and that our lawyers won't."

She was waiting when he was escorted into the room. He immediately gave her a smile, realising perhaps that she was less at ease than he.

"You're looking very attractive, Beth," he said, as soon as he was seated opposite her.

She smiled faintly back at him. "How are things with you, Joe?"

He shrugged. "One day is much the same as another. One just records their arrival and departure and goes on waiting for something different to happen."

"It won't be too long, now, before your trial."

"About two more weeks, I'm told," he murmured abstractedly. "You know, Beth, the awful thing about being in prison is being so dependent on other people. In the normal way if you find yourself in a fix, you work hard to get out of it. But not if you're in prison. If you land there you're utterly dependent on the efforts of others to get you out." He looked distantly into her face. "That's the worst part."

"I'm sure you couldn't have anyone better than Mr. Monk."

"Oh, he's fine. . . . You know he's gone out to Israel? . . . But how ever good your lawyer is—how ever hard your friends are rooting for you—you're impotent to do anything for yourself until the trial starts, when you're suddenly brought up from the dark basement, as it were, and put on display. And if the passers-by don't like what they see, you're pretty soon relegated; though this time for good."

Beth caught the side of her lip with her teeth. She hated to hear him talk like this, to be a witness to this mood of detached despair.

"Everyone in the office is quite *certain* you'll get off," she said vehemently.

"Better tell them not to put any money on it!"

"Joe . . . Joe, don't say things like that, when everyone's doing all they can to help you."

"I don't doubt it, Beth, but I have to face reality. Can enough be done?"

"But you're innocent!"

He gave her a curious little smile which increased her feeling of unease. "That's what the jury's going to decide."

"But how can they convict you if you're innocent?"

"They'll look at the facts, Beth, and they'll say, this chap was involved in a spy racket with the deceased, he now says he saw him killed but he first told the police he was nowhere near the scene, and anyway we know that the man he says did it couldn't have done it, whereas this chap has some of the dead man's blood on one of his shoes, and then there's also that funny business about the stiletto paper-knife missing from his desk. Oh, no, he did it all right." His expression became suddenly determined. "If just one of those links in the chain they've forged against me can be smashed, I'll have a chance. If just one can be . . ."

Beth Steen nodded thoughtfully. "I'm sure more than one will be," she said.

"Let's hope." In a quick change of mood, he asked, "How are things going in the office?"

"Business has been rather quiet, but Femmer's doing a good job. He's an interesting man, too."

"Interesting?" he queried.

Beth blushed. "I've come to know him a bit better since you've been away."

"Oh, I see what you mean."

His tone conveyed nothing, and she felt obliged to explain

further. "I'd always found him rather reserved, but since he's been looking after the business he seems to have been more forth-coming. One wouldn't expect to find a rather gentle, considerate person behind that frozen, mournful expression."

Berg permitted himself the wisp of a smile. "I confess I picked him for his ability rather than his gentle nature or his mournful exterior. However, I'm glad you're getting on all right with him."

"Joe, you haven't misunderstood me, have you?" she said anxiously. "You're . . . you're still the only man in my life."

"Poor Beth, and you've never had more than half of me."

"Anyway, I've had the best half," she said with a small sigh. She wished, however, that the conversation hadn't led them down this particular lane. Her wish was all the stronger as she found herself under his somewhat clinical gaze.

"You'll have to go in a minute," he said abruptly.

"I'll keep in touch with Mr. Monk, Joe, and let him have any-thing which I think could help."

They were now like a couple in that final flurry of messages after the guard has blown his whistle and the train has begun to pull out.

"The stiletto, Beth, if only that could be found."

17

Richard awoke very early that morning. His room was filled with the silent grey light which precedes the actual rising of the sun. There was something mysterious and almost awesome about its quality. He went across and stood by the window, looking out on the utterly motionless scene which stretched away as far as the eye could see. Even the sea gave the appearance of solid pewter.

He returned to his bed and lay there thinking for a quarter of an hour. He thought about Berg on whose behalf he'd come all this way, trying to analyse his belief in his client's innocence. But as on previous occasions he always came back to the same answer. Intuition; which was an unsatisfactory answer to a lawyer. Heaven knows it was a useful characteristic in almost any job, but he felt it should be a guide to careful conduct rather than to quixotic behaviour. Though this, he realised, was Monk, the trained legal mind, wrestling with Monk, the impulsive doer. Well, it was certainly the impulsive doer who had made the journey to Israel, so *he* might as well remain in charge throughout the stay. The trained legal mind could tag along if he wished, and might even be able to contribute a useful comment now and again, but it was clear *he* had, as it were, only come along for the ride.

By the time he had shaved and taken a shower, "room service" had come on duty and he ordered breakfast. While waiting for it to arrive, he dressed and made a tour of his room, reading all the notices that only get read as a last resort by even the most determined time-killers.

Shortly after nine o'clock he telephoned the British Consulate, having first made a fruitless effort to call the Shraga Shipping Company.

"I wanted some information about the Shraga Shipping Company in Eilat Road," he said to the voice that answered at the Consulate. A few seconds later he was explaining his requirement again.

"The Shraga Shipping Company," the new voice repeated vaguely.

"Yes, their office is shut. I wondered if you knew anything about them."

"Can't say I do. In fact, I don't think I've ever heard of that company. Do you have business with them?"

"Yes, I have."

"Well, if you hold on a minute," the voice said doubtfully, "I'll see if I can find out anything for you."

It was a long minute, and Richard began to wonder whether the Consulate hadn't put up its shutters and left him to his own devices. Eventually, however, the voice did return. "Are you still there?"

"I'm afraid so."

"I beg your pardon?" It sounded startled.

"You went away to see if you could find out anything about the Shraga Shipping Company."

"I'm very well aware what I went away for. Furthermore, the answer is very short: I'm afraid we can't help you."

"You mean nobody knows anything about that company?"

"Precisely. They're listed in the telephone book, why don't you try ringing them."

"Because, as I said, they've apparently closed down."

"They don't owe you money, do they?" The voice enquired anxiously.

"Happily not."

" 'Happily' is the word. It crossed my mind you might be involved in some complicated financial transaction with them, but I'm glad for your sake to hear not." By this time the owner of the voice was sounding more buoyant. "I'll make some further enquiries if it'll help, though I can't promise success."

"I'd be grateful. Shall I call you tomorrow morning?"

"All right. Incidentally, I'm afraid I didn't catch your name."

"I haven't given it to anyone. But it's Monk."

"M-O-N-K?"

"That's it."

It wasn't yet ten o'clock and Richard wished he'd told Yuri to come earlier. The lobby of the hotel was full of American tourists and their baggage. They had just debouched from four coaches, and Richard gathered from snatches of overheard conversation that they had come off a ship and were due to make a high-speed tour of the country before embarking three days hence. He mentally wished them well as he steered his way round their mounds of baggage to go out into the garden.

He had just sat down on the terrace overlooking the hotel pool with a cup of coffee, which he didn't particularly want, when Yuri appeared at his side.

"Good morning, Mr. Monk," he said with a bright smile. "I am already here."

"I wasn't expecting you until eleven o'clock."

"I think perhaps your plans become changed, so I come early."

"How did you know about my plans being changed?" Richard enquired with a puzzled smile.

It might have been his imagination, but it seemed that Yuri's expression became suddenly wary.

"Know? I do not know, but plans often are changed, are they not? Also I tell you yesterday that I will arrange with office for car to be reserved for you all day."

"Well, I'm delighted to see you, anyway. It's saved me having to kick my heels for an hour."

"Then you are ready now?"

"I'm ready, Yuri," Richard said, springing to his feet like a soldier falling in on parade. "By the way," he added as they walked towards the car, "I'd like to go to Safad direct. I don't want to make any stops en route."

Yuri gave a perfunctory nod, but for once didn't say anything. Indeed, for the first twenty minutes of the drive he maintained a brooding silence which was in marked contrast with his chattiness of the previous day.

It wasn't until they turned inland from the fertile coastal plain and began to wind through rugged hills covered with olives that his mood changed.

"How long will you stay in Safad, Mr. Monk?" he enquired.

"I shan't know until I've met the person I'm going to see."

"Because I am thinking that I should show you the Sea of Galilee afterwards and we drive back by Mount Tabor and the Valley of Jezreel which is very beautiful."

"If there's time I should enjoy that," Richard said.

"Good. We must make time, I am thinking." He had suddenly become the zestful guide again. "Over there you see an Arab village," he said, waving a hand at a cluster of low, flat-roofed houses on a knoll to their right. "In the Galilee district there are still very many Arabs. And they have much better living than the Arabs in Arab countries. They have the rights and privileges of all citizens who live in Israel. They are well cared for." As the car rounded a bend he pointed at a row of ruined buildings a quarter of a mile away to their left. "That was also an Arab village once, but it was destroyed during the liberation war."

"Why was this village destroyed and the other one not?" Richard asked, gazing at the crumbling walls which were all that was left.

"In this area there was heavy fighting and some villages surrendered and others refused to surrender. It depended on what the mayor told them to do. The ones who didn't fight are now living in peace and prosperity; the others fled, if they were not killed, and they are now living in refugee camps in Syria and Jordan and Lebanon."

Richard decided that an interested nod was sufficient acknowledgement of this rather tendentious remark. But he was not to be that lightly let off.

"You are impressed by what you see in Israel?" Yuri asked.

"Yes, indeed."

"It is fantastical what we have done since 1948." He marvelled awhile in silence at his country's achievements. "Yes, fantastical is the only word."

"How long have you lived in Israel?" Richard enquired.

"I came here in 1938 with my parents. I was only six years old then. I was born in Rumania."

"How many languages can you speak?"

"Hebrew, of course, and Rumanian and French and English and German. But my father could speak seven languages and my mother six, so I am not so good." He threw Richard a grin. "You think I speak fine English."

"Very fine. Where did you learn it?"

"My aunt is married to an Englishman. I should say he was an Englishman, he is now an Israeli."

The car, which had been climbing all this time, rounded a further sharp bend and Yuri exclaimed, "Voilà Safad."

The town was perched on top of a hill, and though it looked no great distance away across the intervening valley, Richard saw that the road to it rose and fell and curved away like a piece of discarded tape.

"Where do you wish to go?" Yuri asked when at last they'd arrived.

"That's the address," Richard said, showing him the piece of paper on which he had written it down and without revealing Berg's name.

"I take it and ask."

A couple of minutes later Yuri returned to the car.

"Your friend is an artist?" he said as they drove off again.

Richard remembered that Berg had disclosed this fact about his brother at their first interview.

"Yes," he replied.

"Safad is a famous artists' colony. When the Arabs left, the government gave their houses to artists. This street is in that quarter. We will leave the car here and I show you where to go."

They had turned into a small, uneven square. A group of

143

tourists were emerging from a mosque, which Yuri informed him had been turned into an art gallery, and were trailing off wearily behind their guide. Yuri pointed up a narrow road which wound out of the square.

"You go up that road and at the top you turn left. You will see the artists have their names outside their houses."

"Will you wait for me here?"

"I wait for you here."

Richard set off up the road. Just before he passed from sight, he looked over his shoulder and saw that Yuri was still standing beside the car and staring after him.

On either side of the road were small, one-storey houses behind white stucco walls. The houses themselves were either white or pale blue. Beside the entrance gate to each was a notice inscribed with the owner's name and an invitation to the passer-by to step inside and inspect his work.

At the top of the ascent the road turned sharply back on itself and narrowed. About twenty yards farther on, he found a sign which read:

Nathan Berg.
Pictures for Sale.
Free inspection. Come in.

There was a wooden gate set in the wall beside the notice and Richard pushed it open and entered. He found himself in a small, wild garden with the house to his left. He wasn't sure whether it was the creeper which hung over much of it or the shutters on the windows, but it had a secretive air. Two paces brought him to the door. There was no sign of a bell or of a knocker, and he rapped on it with his knuckles. Nothing happened and no sound came from inside.

It was all very well saying "Free inspection. Come in", but how was one to avail oneself of the invitation without apparent recourse to burglary?

He rapped on the door a second time, more vigorously than before, but there was still no response. After an interval he walked round to the shaded side of the house where there was a narrow terrace of cracked stones. He reckoned that the whole house couldn't comprise more than three rooms at the most, and that if there was anyone inside they must have heard his knocking on the door. In fact, the house appeared to be completely shut up and the small walled-in garden to be permeated with a thick, sickly sweet silence.

He went up to one of the shuttered windows and was trying to peer into the darkness beyond the crack when a sudden noise behind caused him to swing round. At the same time his heart missed a beat as he raked the area with a searching gaze. But there wasn't a moving creature in sight, and he eventually persuaded himself that it must have been some species of rodent moving in the thick bushes against the wall.

Slowly he turned back to the shuttered window and once more applied his eye to the crack. The next moment he'd leapt away as if an electric current had seized his body, for this time there'd been an eye on the other side. An eye which had stared into his own with unflinching intensity.

Recovering from his shock, he knocked on the shutter and called out, "I want to see Mr. Berg. Is he there?"

With considerable caution he peered through the crack, but the other eye had disappeared. There was a faint sound behind him and he looked round to find an old woman staring at him with a fathomless expression.

A large coarse apron covered a black dress, and she wore a dark blue shawl over her head to frame her face like a nun's. Her skin was the colour of a walnut and deeply wrinkled, and her eyes shone like black diamonds.

"Is Mr. Berg at home?" he enquired, nonplussed by her unremitting gaze.

She shook her head. "Not 'ere," she replied in a deep, gritty voice.

"When will he be back?"

"Evening."

"What time?"

"Six, seven."

Her eyes never left his face as she growled out answers to his questions. However, the main thing was she could understand English, and her demeanour was of minor importance in the circumstances.

"Perhaps I ought to explain," Richard said. "I know Mr. Berg's brother in England and I've come to Safad specially to see Mr. Berg on very important business."

The old woman showed no greater reaction than if he'd regaled her with last Saturday's football results.

"Do you know whether Mr. Berg has received my cables?"

"Mr. Berg not 'ere."

"But he will definitely be here around six or seven this evening?"

"Mr. Berg 'ere evening."

Richard was about to accept defeat when a thought suddenly occurred to him.

"May I see his pictures? The pictures he has for sale?"

This, at least, seemed a way of getting inside the house, though he wasn't quite clear what good that was going to do him.

"No pictures today," she said with finality.

Richard made to walk to the gate. "When Mr. Berg returns, please tell him that I called and will be back this evening. Tell him that it's a matter of great urgency."

He looked at her hopefully, but it was quite impossible to tell how much she understood of what was said to her.

She stood aside to let him pass, and he was about to open the gate into the street when he could have sworn he heard a sound of movement inside the house.

One thing was certain, it couldn't have been the old woman as she was still standing staring at him outside.

Yuri had obviously been watching out for him, as he jumped out of the car and opened the passenger door for Richard as soon as he reappeared in the small square.

"You see your friend?" he asked with undisguised curiosity.

"No, he was out. I shall have to come back at six o'clock. Is it all right to keep you and car till then?"

"It will be all right," Yuri said, though without any enthusiasm. Indeed, he suddenly seemed to be slightly on edge, but he mastered the mood and a moment later said brightly, "And now I drive you to Tiberias on the Sea of Galilee and you can have your lunch."

The drive down to the lakeside was superb, and with his first sight of the lush green Jordan valley Richard could understand just how the hearts of the Children of Israel must have rejoiced when they too received their initial glimpse from the parched hills which lay on either side.

The lake itself was blue and serene in the early afternoon sunshine, and Richard gazed across at the rugged mountains which rose straight up on the eastern shore.

He commented on the scene to Yuri who said, "They are in Syria. It is from there that they sometimes fire on our boats. Then we fire back."

"Where is the actual frontier?"

"You know what, Mr. Monk. On the opposite side where you are looking, thirty feet back from the water only is Israel territory. Beyond that is Syria."

"It looks completely deserted."

"Patrols come there and make provocations."

Richard insisted that Yuri be his guest at lunch, and they had a plain, simple meal at a restaurant of Yuri's recommendation. It was light and airy, and Richard, who didn't feel very hungry, ordered something which turned out to be a sort of cold pancake with a faintly cheesy flavour served with apple purée.

After the meal they drove along the lakeside past the Mount of Beatitudes, which was an unnoteworthy brown slope, to Capernaum, where Yuri insisted Richard get out to look at the Roman ruins. Try though he would, however, his imagination remained unfired and he was glad to sink back into the car again. The trouble was that his mind was too firmly fixed on the outcome of his return visit to Safad to be able also to concentrate on Yuri's flow of biblical history.

"Mount Tabor," Yuri said with a wave of the hand after they had left the Sea of Galilee and been driving south for some time.

Richard rallied his thoughts. "The Transfiguration," he murmured, as though in response to a penny Yuri had put in a slot.

"Yes, and near here Saul consulted the witch of Endor. And in the valley you see over there Gideon fought a big battle." He threw out the name rather as he might have said "Rommel" or "Eisenhower".

"And now I take you to Nazareth."

Richard looked at his watch. It wasn't yet half past three. The time had to be passed somehow, but he could hardly think of less reverential circumstances in which to make a visit to the town in which Our Lord grew up and which bore a name enshrined in so many millions of hearts.

He felt that some spiritual preparation should form part of such

147

a visit, but it was now too late for such and he might just as well be being taken for an afternoon's shopping in Basingstoke for all the uplift he was experiencing.

In the event, he was quite thankful that spiritual preparation had not entered into things as any exaltation of the spirit must surely have been reduced to dismal disappointment by the various holy shrines, which seemed to him to lack everything, save tawdry commercialisation.

"Well?" Yuri greeted him when he emerged from the Grotto of the Annunciation.

Richard could only make a grimace to indicate that he felt a great deal had happened in two thousand years.

After they'd returned to the car, Yuri drove up to the top of one of the surrounding hills from which they had a splendid view of Nazareth nestling below. Richard found that his imagination was now caught by the sense of history which the indoor shrines had failed to evoke. He could picture the story of the New Testament taking place against the landscape beneath his eyes. His own visit to Israel seemed suddenly trivial and unimportant when contemplated in such a perspective. It was with difficulty that he drew himself away from the parapet against which he had been leaning, while his thoughts had roamed across the centuries.

"And now I take you to Afula," Yuri said when they were back in the car.

Richard, who was at that moment studying the map, frowned. "But that's in the opposite direction from Safad."

"We have plenty of time," Yuri replied airily.

"Nevertheless, I'd like to make for Safad now," Richard said in a firm tone.

A shutter came down over Yuri's expression, but he said nothing further. Richard, meanwhile, kept an alert eye on each signpost they came across and from time to time studied the map, which was spread open on his lap. It seemed, however, that whatever he might be thinking Yuri was driving in the right direction.

They had been going for about twenty minutes and were well out in the country when he pulled up at the side of the road. Without a word, he got out and went to the back of the car. He returned in half a minute, shaking his head and making tut-tutting sounds.

"What's wrong?" Richard asked.

"It could be the bearings of the offside rear wheel. It is not good. We must stop at a garage. There is one not far from here."

"How far is Safad?"

"Twenty miles."

"You can call at a garage there while I'm doing my business."

"Safad is too far. It could be dangerous to drive with the wheel in this condition."

He was about to restart the car, when Richard reached a quick decision.

"Let me have a look at it! I know enough about cars to be able to tell whether it's serious or not."

Before Yuri could reply, he had got out and gone round to examine the wheel. So far as he could tell, there was nothing wrong with it at all. However, he called to Yuri to fetch the jack. It would be as well to kill this little diversion as thoroughly as possible. With Yuri standing by in an embarrassed silence, Richard soon had the wheel off and began to examine the brake drum and axle shaft.

"There's nothing wrong with this," he declared. "The bearings are fine. Feel for yourself."

Yuri did so in a half-hearted manner as though he was finding the incident inexpressibly boring.

"And now let's get on to Safad," Richard said determinedly when they were back in the car.

Until this last incident he had been prepared to believe that his doubts about Yuri's behaviour sprang from a mind which was supercharged with suspicion. But now he knew for certain that the doubts were founded in substance. He looked back over the day since the driver had appeared at the hotel to pick him up. There'd been something odd about his manner then. At the time Richard had ascribed it to the normal moodiness of someone who was given that way. Now it had to be seen as the reaction of someone who was playing a particular part. But what part! And played on whose behalf!

The rest of the journey to Safad was accomplished in a grim silence, Yuri neither saying a word, nor so much as giving Richard a sideways glance. His expression remained blank, though, Richard thought he could divine, tinged with concern.

It was dusk when they arrived back in the small uneven square in which they had parked earlier in the day.

"Will you wait for me here?" Richard asked in a strained voice. The atmosphere between them and the build-up of his own thoughts had done nothing to erase the growing feeling of tension within him at the unknown prospect ahead.

"I wait," Yuri said, staring studiously through the windscreen in front of him.

Just before Richard reached the bend which would take him out of sight of the car, he looked back, but it was too dark to discern whether Yuri was watching him or not.

He reached Berg's gate and stood on tiptoe to peer over the top. No light came from within the house. He almost expected to find the gate bolted against him, but it was not, and he entered. He closed it quickly and stood gazing for a moment at the dark outline of the house. The darkness seemed to add to the all-pervading silence, and he glanced up at the sky as if a supplicant. The last traces of daylight were almost gone and the whole vast dome above was already pricked by a thousand stars.

He stood rooted just inside the gate trying to decide what his course should be. Would it be better to make a stealthy reconnaissance or to walk up to the door and rap boldly on it? A second's thought satisfied him that the second course was the one to follow. After all, he was calling on legitimate business and he'd best behave like a normal visitor.

It seemed to him as he knocked on the door that the noise echoed like thunder in the valley. But once the sound had died away in his own ears, silence was once more complete.

As he stood there wondering what to do next, he knew for certain that unknown forces were pitted against him, that Nathan Berg's absence was no mischance, but a deliberate thwart. He began to feel angry. He'd come the hell of a way just to have a door firmly shut in his face. And anyway it wasn't his face, it was Joseph Berg's face. He was the man who stood to suffer through the anonymous conspiracy which mocked at his solicitor.

He walked round the side of the house to the shuttered window through which the old woman had eyed him that morning. So far as he could see the whole house was in darkness. Not a sign of light came from anywhere inside. Could it be that the occupants, whoever they might be, were sitting there in darkness waiting for him to give up his quest and go? He suddenly decided that he hadn't come all the way from England to be put off as easily as that. How could he possibly return home and tell everyone "Well, I did knock on the door, but nobody answered"? He'd never be able to lift his head again. No, he had to do something to justify his journey. Something to show his unknown opponents that he wasn't that soft and easy to deter. The question was how best could he make a satisfactory nuisance of himself!

He was still pondering over the possibilities when he heard a footfall behind. Before he had time to turn, he was rugger-tackled and sent flying into the bushes at the end of the terrace. His assailant who crashed on top of him added a few body punches for good measure before getting up and vanishing.

Slowly and painfully, Richard disentangled himself from the bush and stood up. His shoulder throbbed and one hand felt as though it had been crushed in a steel mill. Mentally he took stock of himself and was surprised to discover that he still appeared to be of one piece. While he did so, he remained crouching warily against the bush, waiting for the enemy's next move. For what was quite certain was that his attacker still lurked somewhere in the garden. He'd have heard the click of the gate if the man had left. He was probably hiding not more than three or four yards away, which could only mean that a further assault was intended.

"Bastard!" Richard shouted out suddenly into the dark night. The unfairness of the attack riled him more than the physical hurt he'd sustained. He reckoned he could give a reasonable account of himself in any normal shindig, but to be caught from behind and projected unceremoniously into a spiky bush was an affront to dignity as much as anything else.

"Bloody bastard!" he shouted out again.

A twig snapped just behind him and the next second a pair of powerful arms had been locked round his body. Powerless to use his own hands, he kicked out viciously with his right heel and connected with a shin. There was a grunt of pain, but the grip in which he was being held didn't for one second slacken. Indeed, it became tighter so that he almost expected to hear his own ribs crack under the colossal pressure. The man behind him must be a giant. As if to confirm this judgment, he was suddenly lifted right off his feet and carried bodily. At the same time a second pair of hands gripped his legs and he was borne across to the gate with no more difficulty than if he'd been a wriggling puppy.

One of the men opened the gate and the next thing Richard was aware of was of sailing through the air. The sensation, however, was short-lived and he landed in a full-length crash on the broken surface of the road.

Afterwards, he could definitely remember landing, but then things had begun to spin wildly before his eyes and he'd felt even sicker than he had once on the giant dipper when gorged with chocolate éclairs.

He didn't know how long he lay there, but guessed it wasn't in fact much more than two minutes. When consciousness returned he still felt terribly sick, but with an effort he stood up and went and leant against a wall.

There was no sign of life from Berg's house and the gate was shut. His two assailants were presumably waiting to see whether he returned and, if so, to repeat their message that he wasn't wanted.

Limping painfully, he made his way back to the square, stopping every so often to take a deep breath and summon up the strength required for every step.

Yuri must have been watching for him, as he came running up with an expression of anxious concern and put a supporting arm round his shoulder. Neither of them spoke while Yuri, now as attentive as a nurse, helped him into the car and put a cushion for his head.

They had been driving for a quarter of an hour before Richard, who had been thinking as hard as his still dazed mind would allow, said, "You weren't surprised, were you?"

"Please?"

"You knew I was going to be beaten up, didn't you?"

"How should I know such a thing?"

His tone, however, lacked conviction, and Richard decided he must find out the truth whatever the cost to his already splitting head.

"If you didn't actually know it was going to happen, you certainly weren't surprised to see that it had." He paused. "Were you?" But Yuri drove on in silence, staring embarrassedly ahead. "Were you?" Richard repeated.

"It is not wise to talk about these things, Mr. Monk," he said suddenly in a pleading tone.

"There's only you and I in the car, so wisdom doesn't enter into it. It's important that I know and, in the circumstances, I think the least you can do is to tell me. After all, in a sense you led me into the trap."

"No, no, not true," Yuri expostulated.

"You let me walk into it, anyhow."

Yuri shook his head vigorously. "No, I was worried for you. I did not want anything to happen."

"But you weren't surprised when it did!"

"No, it is true I was not surprised," he said in a dejected whisper. "I was warned. . . ."

"Start at the beginning and tell me the lot."

Yuri was silent for a couple of minutes. "If I tell you, will you promise not to betray me?"

"If you mean, will I promise not to tell others what you've told me, yes, I will promise."

A pause ensued while Yuri negotiated the overtaking of a truck which was hogging the crown of the road.

"When I went to the office after leaving you at the hotel last night, I was told the manager wanted to see me. In his room there is a man I have not seen before. He does not tell me his name, but after the manager has gone, he asks me about you. I tell him that I have fetched you from Lod Airport as instructed and taken you to the hotel. He asks what we talked about and I tell him that I point out all the interesting things to you. He then ask what you going to do next and I say that I drive you to Safad today and he say 'Ha!' and become very interested. He ask if I know why you want to go to Safad and I tell him 'No'; your business is not my business and I mind my own business when driving visitors. After that, he tell me you go to visit a certain person in Safad, but you not wanted there and it better if you don't go. I say to him, how can I stop him; he tell me to drive him to Safad and he pay. I cannot tell him not to go to Safad. So the man shrugs and says it is difficult for me, but, if possible, not to drive you to Safad. It will not be a helpful journey for you. So I say to the man, why do *you* not tell Mr. Monk not to go to Safad? But he says that it not convenient and if you go, you go, but there may be difficulties for you. He says there will be men in Safad who may be disagreeable when they see you."

"You can say that again," Richard remarked with feeling.

"And that is all I can tell you, Mr. Monk. I promise I do not know any more."

"And you have no idea who this man was?"

Yuri shook his head. "Afterwards, I ask the manager, but he just said he didn't know either, but he was an official."

"Can you guess what sort?"

"Yes, I can guess," Yuri said almost eagerly. "I think he was a security policeman."

"I think you're probably right," Richard said.

"And you are one, too?"

"As it happens, I'm not. But if I were, I'd still say I wasn't."

Yuri looked puzzled and Richard left him that way. It was now quite clear that the roughing up he had received had been by way of an official warning to keep away from Nathan Berg. He also now understood why there'd been no response to his letters or cables. He could see how his arrival had, in the circumstances, brought out the strong-arm boys of the security service. He knew that every country maintained its official emissaries who could be relied upon for effective unofficial action when the state's interest required it—or rather when an anonymous bod decided that the state interest required it.

Yuri broke in on his thoughts. "You will not tell what I have said?" he enquired anxiously.

"I've already given you my promise."

"That was before."

"Then I give it to you again now."

Yuri smiled. "An Englishman's word is always his bond, is it not so?"

Richard smothered the somewhat cynical retort which came into his mind and merely nodded. This in itself was not exactly a ringing response to the question.

When they arrived back at the hotel, he had the utmost difficulty in getting out of the car, his maltreated joints having stiffened during the journey. A startled expression crossed the face of the concierge who handed him his key.

"You have an accident, sir?" he asked, looking Richard up and down.

"Yes, but it appears worse than it was," Richard replied hurriedly. It was not a moment for explanations, even untruthful ones.

154

As soon as he reached his room, he undressed and drew a long, hot bath. As he lay wallowing, he reflected that hot baths must surely make up a small part of heaven. Nothing on earth had yet been invented which was more deliciously soothing.

One by one he examined his injuries, satisfying himself that, uncomfortable though they were, no actual bones seemed to have been broken. One ankle was swollen and there was a long graze the whole length of the same leg. His shoulder on that side of the body was extremely tender to the touch and was beginning to turn a storm-cloud colour. There were a number of scratches all over his face, presumably from the bush into which he had been flung head-first. But none of these were serious, though they might incline him to grow a beard, since their presence was not going to make shaving a very enjoyable experience. Finally, he could feel a lump on the back of his head, which he must have sustained when he landed in the road. It led him to wonder what his assailants would have done if he'd died there and then of a fractured skull. Probably carted his body away and dumped it in a place known for its footpads. "English tourist robbed and left dying"—he could see the headline clearly.

After his bath, he took two aspirin and got into bed. The question now was, what to do next. His adversaries might have succeeded in battering his body, but they hadn't dented his determination. If anything, their crude efforts had merely served to increase it.

He hadn't reached any decision, however, when he drifted into an exhausted sleep.

He woke up with a start to find the sun already high in the sky. For a split second he wondered what it was that had awakened him, and then the telephone near his head rang again.

He reached for it and winced as the manoeuvre brought him leaning on his bruised shoulder.

"Hello." His voice was no more than a sleepy croak.

"Do I speak to Mr. Monk?"

"Yes, Monk speaking." He wriggled himself into a more comfortable position.

"My name is Nathan Berg, Mr. Monk." Though the English was perfect, the voice had a thickness of timbre. Richard pictured its owner as a formidable sort of person. This was not the voice of a nervous light-weight.

"I'm glad to hear from you, Mr. Berg. I've had a fairly strenuous time trying to get in touch with you."

"I know you have and I'm sorry for it, even though it was unavoidable. I'm 'phoning you as it'll be our only chance of speaking. I may say that I shan't be very popular if it's ever discovered that I've been in touch with you, but that's a risk I'm willing to take."

"Did you receive my letters?"

"Yes, but I'm afraid I was under instructions not to answer them."

"Anyhow, you know what's brought me to Israel?"

"It might be best if I explain quickly why I'm 'phoning you, Mr. Monk. It is to say that I'm very sorry to hear of my brother's trouble, but there's nothing I can do to help. If you wonder why I've taken the trouble to emerge from obscurity just to tell you that, it's because, strange though it may sound, I feel I owe you something for what you're doing—and have gone through—on his behalf, and because our blood tie requires me to express personally my concern for my brother's position."

"But not to go any further than that?"

"I've already gone further than I'm allowed."

"What you're saying is that so-called duty to your country comes before family feeling?"

If Richard had hoped in this way to taunt him into affording greater assistance, he was quickly disappointed.

"Yes," Berg replied. "In this particular instance, I'm afraid it does, though I hope this 'phone call won't send you away entirely empty-handed."

"Well?"

"I gather you're anxious to confirm that my brother played only a minor part in the activities in which he was engaged—voluntarily engaged, let me make it quite clear."

"He doesn't pretend otherwise."

"Good! Anyway, the answer is that he acted as nothing more than a post office. He was, shall I say, a small and, in a sense, mechanical link in a chain of communication. He had nothing to do with the collection of information or with its ultimate use. He was a cypher. As I said, I have no right to be talking to you at all, but I thought the least I could do was to tell you what I have. Also"—his tone took on a note of sardonic amusement—"there was no knowing what you mightn't get up to next, it being very clear that persistence is one of your characteristics." He paused. "I'm sufficiently well aware of the English rules of evidence to know that you won't be able to quote me in open court or make official use of what I've told you, but nevertheless I hope my call has been more useful than otherwise."

Richard was silent for a moment, as he thought over what Berg had told him.

"What was the value of the information he was passing? It could be very important to be able to show that it wasn't vital stuff. Vital that is to our national interest."

"I'm afraid I can't help you at all over that. Not at all."

"And what about the Shraga Shipping Company?"

"Just a letter-box."

"And you, Mr. Berg?"

"Me? I'm an artist, making a not very successful living."

"And what do you do besides painting pictures?"

"That's neither here nor there."

"And that's all you can tell me?"

"Surely, it's what you wanted to know. I'm sorry I can't let you have it in the form of a signed statement, but you must be satisfied with what you've got. Tell me, Mr. Monk, what are my brother's chances?"

"Fifty-fifty."

"Is that lawyer's caution?"

"No, it's a fair assessment. I personally believe in his innocence but the dice are loaded fairly heavily against him and his defence is not made easier by the conspiracy of silence which binds you and your like."

Berg ignored this rebuke. "I should be grateful if you would write and let me know the result of his trial."

"All right. I can't help hoping that, should he be convicted, you'll feel it on your conscience."

"That's understandable. Your hope, I mean. And now I really must ring off. Incidentally, I ought to have said this at the outset, I hope you weren't shaken up too badly yesterday. I personally very much regret that you were subjected to physical violence, but I'm afraid I was given no say in the matter."

"It certainly wasn't the fault of your two friends that I'm not now in hospital with two broken legs and a ruptured spleen. Throwing people through the air so that they land heavily on a hard surface never improves them."

"You mayn't believe me, Mr. Monk, but I can only say again that I'm very sorry." In the brief silence which followed, Richard had the impression that Berg was trying to make up his mind whether to say something further. It was in a take-it-or-leave-it tone that he suddenly added, "It might be worth your while when you get home to look for someone called Fanos. I say *it might*, because I don't know any more, so it's no good your asking me."

In fact, he gave Richard no chance to, as a second later he had rung off. Richard looked at his watch and saw that it was just after nine o'clock. Though he was infernally stiff and sore, he felt a very different person from the previous night, and reflected on the restorative properties of a night's sleep.

As he sat in the window eating his breakfast, he gave his mind to his next step. The more he thought about it, the more he realised that Nathan Berg had, in fact, answered the main points which had brought him to Israel. There had probably been small chance anyway of bringing him or any other witness all the way to London merely to say that Joseph Berg was only a minor cog in a very large machine. As to the value of the information which was being passed, this could hardly be in the top, top secret category when, in fact, it was deliberate misinformation. False information being fed to the Egyptians with a tip-off to the Israelis. It was difficult to see whose national interest had suffered apart from the Egyptians'. In a sense it could be seen as a contest between the intelligence services of those two states, with England, as it were, having provided the pitch but nothing further. On the other hand, he could see that the security service at home might not care for the fact that the pitch had been hired out without their knowledge. After all, it was *their* pitch. As to Fanos, what was he supposed to do about that tossed-out name? Search Soho?

By the time he had finished his breakfast he'd decided that the sooner he returned home the better. Nothing further would be gained by staying on. He 'phoned down to the travel desk in the hotel and made a reservation on a direct flight that left Lod at half-past four in the afternoon. Next, he ordered a car to drive him there.

"If you like to leave around eleven, Mr. Monk, you could visit Caesarea on the way," the clerk said. "You should really see it. It is of double historical interest. There are the Roman ruins of biblical times and the relics of a Crusader fortress city of a thousand years later. I think you will find it very interesting. I will arrange it for you, yes?"

"I'm sure I ought to go there, but not today," Richard said apologetically. "I had an accident yesterday and I can't walk very well."

"That is too bad. Next time then, yes?"

"Next time, for certain."

"Very well, I will arrange the car for two o'clock to drive you direct to Lod."

"I'll be ready."

When he did present himself at the travel desk shortly before two, the young lady in charge looked at him with a long, unhappy face.

"I have a confession to make, Mr. Monk. I hope you will not be very cross."

Richard braced himself for the worst, which could only be that fate had planted one of the customary obstacles with which she besets the traveller—and especially the traveller by air—meaning that he would be obliged to stay on an extra night.

"All the drivers are very busy today," she went on in breathless apology, "and there is only one left. But as you were going direct to the airport, I thought you would not perhaps be too angry. You are not, I hope?"

"Angry about what?" Richard asked, mystified.

The girl, in turn, looked mystified for a second, then let out a small screech. "But of course I have not told you about him. He cannot speak English."

She looked at him anxiously.

"Is that all that's wrong with him?"

"Oh, yes. He is a very good driver."

"Then I'll let you into a secret. I'm delighted to hear he can't speak English."

"Delighted! But you should not be delighted. You will miss much which he cannot tell you."

Richard felt unable to explain that this was precisely what he meant.

One day he'd come back to Israel on a proper holiday, but, in the meantime, all he wanted was to get out of it with the minimum of fuss.

He arrived at Lod Airport with over an hour to spare. The place wore the desultory air which settles over smaller airports between the bursts of activity which are precipitated by the arrival or departure of a plane. He decided that he might as well clear Customs and Immigration straight away. That done, he'd feel one step nearer home.

The officer to whom he handed his passport glanced up sharply. "One moment, please," he said and disappeared abruptly through a door, taking the passport with him. Before a nonplussed Richard had time to feel either frightened or angry, the door re-opened and the officer beckoned to him.

Sitting behind a desk in a small, excessively stuffy room was a middle-aged man in a crumpled open-neck shirt. Despite needing a shave and looking tired, he had an air of authority. He motioned Richard to a chair.

"You're returning to England?" he asked, idly turning the pages of the passport. His English bore only the slightest traces of an accent.

"Yes, by the B.E.A. flight in an hour's time."

The man nodded slowly. "It would have been better still if you hadn't come, Mr. Monk."

"I've already received the message that I'm not exactly a popular visitor."

"Does that surprise you? After all, every country tries to guard its intelligence operations against prying eyes and . . . well, the bumbling amateur can be the biggest nuisance of all. Especially, the tenacious one. And you, Mr. Monk, fit all of that description."

"Since, presumably, you know the reason for my visit, I should like to say that everyone could have been saved a lot of trouble if you'd allowed me the information I sought. Then I wouldn't have had to bumble—as you put it—so much."

"Ah, but it's not as easy as that. Nothing ever is, of course," he added with a sigh. "It so happens that you were rubbing against a particularly sensitive nerve in your efforts to see Mr. Nathan Berg. For reasons that don't concern you, but which

160

have nothing to do with the purpose of your visit, it would have been very undesirable for you to have met him."

"Undesirable for who? The art world of Israel?" Richard inquired sarcastically. "You don't have to be so coy. I realise Nathan Berg is one of your secret agents."

"Nathan Berg is a painter. It would be as well for you to remember that when you get home."

"O.K., have it that way if you want," Richard replied with a touch of impatience. "Anyway, I didn't seek this little interview, you did. It's about time you came to the point."

The man smiled for the first time. "That's simple, Mr. Monk. It was decided that someone should see you officially off the premises and repeat the warning not to interfere in our corner of the cabbage patch." He rose from his chair and pulled his damp clinging shirt away from his body. "Sometimes in our line of business we co-operate with one another at a professional level; other times, not. This is a *not* occasion. But the one thing none of us in the trade ever does is to take outsiders into our confidence. At least, unless compelled by force majeur. And I'm afraid you're an outsider in this matter, as far as we're concerned."

"So I'm a bumbling amateur and an outsider, am I!" Richard observed grimly.

The man's smile broadened. "Well, just take a look at yourself in a mirror, Mr. Monk!"

Before Richard could reply, he'd walked across and opened the door. "Ah, here's your plane coming in now. Don't forget your passport. . . ."

Richard limped out and the door immediately closed behind him. There were no handshakes, no good-byes. As he made his way to the departure lounge, he found a grain of satisfaction in the fact that the man had obviously been unaware of Nathan Berg's telephone call that morning. So much for his infuriating air of omnipotence!

18

At about the same time as Richard's plane became airborne that afternoon, Detective-Superintendent Kettleman poked his head round the door of his Detective-Inspector's room.

Since Berg's committal for trial, he had been largely occupied with another investigation and had left Inspector Evans in charge of the few remaining matters which needed attention, most of them points which were automatically dealt with in the course of pre-trial routine. He had merely kept in touch with events and been available for consultation when his D.I. thought advisable.

"Anything new?" he enquired, looking at the neatly arranged piles of paper which covered Inspector Evans's desk to make it resemble a stationery counter. He only wants to put price tags on them to complete the illusion, he thought.

"Monk's gone to Israel," Evans said. "Inspector Pullar was on the 'phone half an hour ago and told me."

Kettleman was thoughtful for a second, then shrugged. "And what good is that supposed to be going to do him?"

"Pullar didn't know."

"If he doesn't, I certainly don't. Anyhow, why doesn't he know? I thought these security boys spent their time hopping in and out of one another's pockets."

"I rather gathered that our people hadn't got very far in unearthing Berg's overseas contacts. They've run up against a brick wall."

"As far as I'm concerned, they can run into the Great Wall of China. We've got a perfectly good case of murder against Berg and it doesn't hinge on the subterranean tremors of anyone's security service."

"It would still be nice to know why Monk made his journey."

"If Pullar asks nicely, he'll probably tell him," Kettleman remarked scathingly as he departed to his own room.

Richard had sent a cable to Sheila giving his flight details and asking her to arrange for a car to meet him at London Airport. To his surprise and considerable pleasure, however, Alan's was the first face he saw as he limped away from Customs Inspection. As his own face lit up, so Alan's assumed an expression of consternation.

"What on earth's happened to you, Richard? Have you been shot up or something?"

"Or something," Richard replied with a rueful grin. "I'll explain when we're in the car. Incidentally, I take it you have come to meet *me*?"

"Yes, I happened to 'phone Sheila to ask if she'd had any news from you and she'd just received your cable. So I told her I'd meet you. She never mentioned you were a 'walking wounded'."

"I didn't put it in the cable."

Alan carried Richard's bag to the car and became almost as solicitous as Yuri had been the previous evening.

The previous evening! It seemed quite incredible that it was little over twenty-four hours before that he had been beaten up in a place called Safad in the hills of Galilee. Driving now up the M4 to London, surrounded by familiar landmarks, the events of yesterday, even of this very morning, assumed a detached remoteness. Indeed, were it not for the physical reminders, he would have been tempted to have believed that it had all happened to someone else and that he had merely been enjoying a vicarious experience. But there was nothing vicarious about the swellings to his head and shoulder.

By the time he had finished telling Alan everything, they'd arrived outside his flat.

"Come in and have a drink," Richard said.

"I reckon I might even beat you at squash now," Alan remarked pleasantly as he watched him limping around the living-room.

"About your only chance!"

With Berg's trial only ten days off, it was inevitable that their conversation soon turned back to this topic.

"What we now have to decide," Richard said, "is whether Berg *would* be well advised to make a full statement to the police at this stage about his part in the spying activities."

"I know, I've been thinking about it while you've been away, Richard. I don't believe he would. I can't see where the advantage lies, especially as the prosecution are not in any position to disprove what our chap says about himself. It's not as though they can call evidence that he played a much bigger part than he says. In those circumstances, I think it would be better tactics to say nothing until the trial. Let his appearance in the witness-box be the first time when he gives his account."

"It's just a question of whether the jury mightn't feel that someone who was as lightly implicated as he says wouldn't have taken an earlier opportunity of telling the police."

"I know, but I still adhere to my view. After all, it wasn't until the preliminary hearing that we knew the prosecution was going to advance the spying motive. That being so, we're entitled to keep back our reply until Berg himself gives evidence. It's only in exceptional circumstances that a defendant makes a statement to the police between committal and trial. When, for example, there's some particular reason for his wanting to establish an element of his defence in advance. I can't see that there's any such particular reason in this case. As it is the prosecution seem to be pretty much in the dark as to the part he did play. If we start telling them before the trial, it'll only give them something to work on."

Richard nodded. "I can see the force of that. Moreover, my trip to Israel tends to support that viewpoint."

"Quite."

"The other major decision we have to make concerns the Gamel angle."

"That's a bloody Morton's fork if ever there was one!" Alan said with feeling. "If Berg insists on saying in the witness-box that Gamel murdered Parsons, the prosecution are obviously going to seek to call rebutting evidence."

"We might be able to resist that."

"Certainly we'll try, but suppose we don't succeed. You remember what Paul Prentice said to us during the lunch adjournment: that he had evidence available to show that Gamel could not have committed the murder."

"According to Berg, there must be a flaw in it somewhere," Richard remarked helplessly.

"I know he says that, but how the hell can we begin to prove it until we know what the evidence consists of in detail. And, anyway, there's no guarantee we'll be able to prove it then. We just have to face the possibility that their evidence is cast-iron on the impossibility of Gamel having committed the crime. And if that's so, our whole defence will backfire with the direst consequences."

There was a silence while each pondered his own thoughts.

"Of course," Richard said slowly, "Berg had never met Gamel. He has only assumed from what Parsons had told him that Gamel must have been the murderer."

"Because he knew Parsons was going to meet Gamel that Friday evening," Alan broke in. "And that's what Berg will say in the witness-box. So that even if he admits he can't say of his own personal knowledge that Gamel was the murderer, he's going to point the finger strongly in his direction. And once he does that and the prosecution play their trump, he's had it." Alan shook his head wearily from side to side. "It'll scarcely be open to us to say to the jury, 'Well, he must have made a mistake; however, if it wasn't Gamel, then it was someone else. Afraid we can't suggest who, but definitely it wasn't Mr. Berg.' And that's the dead end into which we'll be forced if we're not careful."

"Once the jury accept that some not-very-glamorous spying activities form the background of this case, surely they can be persuaded to accept that all sorts of unknown persons were inevitably also involved and that it could just as well have been one of them who killed Parsons."

"That's what I call trying to make bricks without straw, Richard. The trouble is that the prosecution did have sufficient straw to make a reasonable brick and it has BERG written all over it. On the other hand I agree that we may be driven to suggest something of the sort to the jury. I think that when the time comes it may be best to keep all our options open until the last possible moment. It'll be one of those defences that one has to play by ear."

"And what about this name Berg threw at me at the last moment?"

"Fanos?" Alan made a face. "All we can do is mention it to Pullar and see if it means anything to him."

The telephone rang and Richard hobbled across to answer it.

"Oh, hello, Sheila.... Yes, Mr. Scarby met me all right.... I got in about half an hour ago. ... Oh yes, what did she want? ... Well, thanks for ringing, anyway, Sheila. I'll see you in the morning."

He turned to Alan and said, "Sheila says that Miss Steen telephoned this afternoon in a state of great excitement."

"What was she excited about?"

"Sheila gathered that the missing paper-knife had been found."

19

Berg's trial opened at the Old Bailey on a Wednesday ten days later. The preceding days had been busy ones for Richard, with visits to his client in Brixton Prison and two long conferences with Alan which led to yet further activity on the part of his instructing solicitor.

Berg had accepted Richard's account of his visit to Israel philosophically. He had been quite touchingly distressed to learn of the violence to which he'd been subjected, but, when it came to it, hadn't seemed as upset about his brother's attitude as Richard had expected. Indeed, it was noticeable that he had become fatalistically resigned to whatever might be about to befall him. If he still hoped for the best, he was certainly prepared for the worst. The time he had already spent in custody, awaiting trial, had wrought that change in his outlook. He was like a wild bird trapped in a room. The feverish flutterings of endeavour became slowly less and were replaced by an erosive apathy. It was worrying, and Richard did everything he could think of to counter it. He came to the conclusion that the break-up of his marriage, which the case had not so much caused as given the final wrench to, was more responsible than any other factor for this dangerous apathy.

On the Monday before the trial began, Richard received through the post a large brown envelope which he could see had emanated from the Director of Public Prosecutions Department. Inside, as he had immediately suspected, was a document known as a Notice of Additional Evidence.

The frontispiece informed him that in addition to the witnesses who had been called at the Magistrates' Court the prosecution was proposing to call others whose evidence was attached. He quickly turned the pages of the document and saw that it related solely to Gamel's death.

Apart from the evidence of Mrs. Cluff about her lodger's movements—or rather lack of them—on the fatal Friday evening, there was formal evidence to prove that her lodger, Mr. Fawzi, was in fact Mr. Gamel, and lastly evidence of a pathologist (the same Dr. Lancaster who had performed the post-mortem examination of Parsons) to the effect that Gamel had died of bar-biturate poisoning; as a result of a heavy overdose of sleeping tablets.

Richard telephoned Alan in Chambers to give him the news.

"Can't say I'm surprised," Alan remarked. "It's an astute move on their part, nevertheless. I mean, if we don't pursue the Gamel line in cross-examination, they won't have to call that evidence unless we require them to, which we shouldn't in those circumstances. On the other hand if we do pursue the Gamel line, then they can call their additional witnesses to deal with the point."

"And without running the risk of a judge refusing them permission to call it in rebuttal on the close of our case," Richard added.

"Exactly. Which he might have done seeing that the Gamel defence has partially adumbrated. In such circumstances he might well have said that the prosecution oughtn't to have been taken by surprise and that consequently he wouldn't allow them to call rebutting evidence at that stage."

"I'll get a copy of the notice to you by midday, Alan."

"Thanks, Richard. I'll give you a call this evening when I've considered it in detail."

The next evening Richard attended a final conference with Alan and at half-past ten on Wednesday morning the trial began.

Mr. Justice Harris, one of the judges of middle rank seniority, had been assigned to try the case. Alan, who had appeared before him on a number of occasions, liked and respected him. His had been one of those judicial appointments which had taken the profession largely by surprise, but which had since received unreserved approbation. He had a reputation for fairness and non-interruption, and that, most members of the Bar felt, was as much as you could ask of any trial judge.

Number One Court was crowded when he took his seat. Berg came up the stairs into the enormous dock which filled the centre of the court-room and, stepping briskly to the front, gave the judge a small formal bow.

"Always wish they wouldn't do that," Alan leant over to whisper in Richard's ear. "It looks so affected."

"I don't see that it's any more affected than bowing to him just after he's given you ten years, and a lot of them do that too."

167

"I jolly well know I wouldn't in the circumstances," Alan whispered back. "Try and spit in his eye perhaps, but not bow."

Alan was sitting at the opposite end of the row from prosecuting counsel, with Richard immediately in front of him at the large table which filled the well of the court. By getting up and standing on tiptoe it would just be possible for Richard to hold whispered conversations with his client several feet above, provided he leaned forward over the front ledge of the dock. It was a situation which would have been tolerable only to Romeo and Juliet.

While the jury was being sworn, the lawyers sorted their papers for the umpteenth time or gazed about them with the air of professional insouciance expected of them by the lay public.

The conduct of the prosecution was now in the hands of Mr. Green and Mr. Hyslop, two of the Treasury Counsel who handled crown cases at the Old Bailey.

Just before Green rose to open the case to the jury, he slid along the row and said to Alan: "You've seen the notice of additional evidence?"

"Yes."

"Have you any views on whether I should open that evidence to the jury, Alan?"

"What you mean is, am I going to plug the Gamel defence?"

"Precisely."

"I don't think I can help you, Stephen. You must act as you think best."

"So be it," Green said without malice, sliding back to his own end of the row.

In the event, he opened the case in almost identical fashion to that in which Prentice had outlined it to Mr. Chaplin in the Magistrates' Court, save that he went into considerably more detail.

For the rest of the day the witnesses came and went, with Alan cross-examining to the same purpose as he had on the previous occasion. If the public had expected high drama, they were disappointed. So far it was a fight with kid gloves on. When Richard mentioned this impression to Alan at the end of the first day's hearing, he had said, "The gloves will be off tomorrow all right," and they had both grinned in a knowing fashion.

The first witness to be called the next morning was Miss Parrot. She looked even more frightened than she had in Mr. Chaplin's court and her voice, which had been barely audible there, produced fewer sound waves than a canary drinking.

Alan watched with forensic satisfaction as she became whiter and more rigid with every exhortation to speak up. He realised, however, that though judge and counsel were becoming slowly exasperated, the jury could be transmitting a collective wave of sympathetic understanding to a fellow stranger.

Eventually Green sat down and mopped his face, which was damp from his exertions in eliciting her evidence.

When Alan rose to cross-examine she gazed at him like a rabbit which, having survived the ferret, finds itself confronted by a snake.

"Miss Parrot," he said in a deliberately gentle tone, "do you recall telling me in the Magistrates' Court that so far as you were concerned, anything might have happened to the paper-knife which Mr. Berg used to keep in his drawer?"

"I think so," she replied in a cautious whisper.

"Then it wouldn't surprise you to hear that it has been found again?" The witness merely stared at Alan who said in a slightly firmer tone, "Well, would it?"

"Would it?" she repeated stupidly.

"Would it surprise you?"

"I suppose not."

"I'd like you to look at this paper-knife, Miss Parrot," Alan said as Richard produced it, like a conjurer, from his briefcase and handed it to the usher who put it on the ledge of the witness-box.

The court became suddenly still, as coughing and shuffling were suspended at what was quickly felt to be the first moment of palpable drama. Prosecuting counsel became doubly alert, and the judge fixed both witness and exhibit with an unwavering gaze.

"Do you recognise that paper-knife, Miss Parrot?" Alan asked, leaning forward to add emphasis to his words.

"It's like Mr. Berg's," she said falteringly.

"Could it be the one you've described?"

"I don't know," she whispered.

"Is it in any way different from it?"

"I don't think it is."

"It's the same then?"

"Yes."

"Very well, I'll ask you again. Could that paper-knife on the ledge in front of you be Mr. Berg's?"

"I suppose it could."

"Thank you, Miss Parrot, that's all I want to ask you."

Turning to the judge, Alan said, "I shall of course be calling evidence, my lord, as to the finding of that exhibit."

"Very well, Mr. Scarby."

As he sat down, Alan was pleased to see the prosecution team bending their heads together in huddled consultation. "Surprise number one for the other side," he murmured to Richard, who grinned.

By the time the luncheon adjournment was reached, only the police evidence remained to be called.

"And now," Alan said, as he bit into a ham sandwich at the public house to which they'd gone for a quick snack, "our decision can be deferred no longer. Do we run the Gamel line or don't we?"

"I thought we'd settled that."

"It's not too late to change our minds."

"I see no reason to."

"Good, nor do I, but I wanted to make sure that you still agreed. Then we leave it strictly alone."

"As far as I'm concerned, the notice of additional evidence clinched it. If we had anything on which to cross-examine it might be different, but let's not give them any excuse to call that extra stuff."

"Agreed, Richard."

"Incidentally, I've had a word with Pullar and the name Fanos means nothing at all to him."

Alan accepted the information with a gallic shrug and downed the rest of his beer.

Shortly before four o'clock that afternoon Green stood up and informed the judge that the prosecution had completed its evidence.

"I have a copy of a notice of additional evidence here, Mr. Green," the judge said, fingering the document with fastidious care.

"It was served on my instructions, my lord, but as matters have turned out, I don't think it lies open to me to argue its relevance."

"I'm glad you take that view since I would feel bound to hold that its content is wholly irrelevant as the case stands." He glanced at Alan. "I take it, Mr. Scarby, that you're not insisting that this evidence should be called."

"No, my lord," Alan said firmly.

"Very well, we'll adjourn now until tomorrow morning."

Richard was pleased to note that when Alan rose to open the defence case to the jury the next morning he immediately had their interested attention. He had obviously impressed them as someone worth listening to.

He told them that he didn't intend to address them at any length since they would shortly be hearing the full defence case from the lips of Berg and his witnesses, and that it would come much better from them than from him.

He then went on: "Members of the jury, you now know from what I have told you that there is very little conflict between the prosecution and the defence, save on the vital issue of who murdered Parsons. The prosecution have presented a set of circumstances before you and invited you to draw as an inescapable inference that Berg killed Parsons. The defence will present a set of facts very little different in substance and invite you to say that that is not an inescapable inference and that the prosecution have not satisfied you beyond a reasonable doubt that Berg must —I repeat *must*—have been the murderer.

"He will admit to you that he lied to the police when they first called on him and, of course, the prosecution lay great stress on that lie and suggest that only a man with a guilty secret to hide would lie in such circumstances. Well, as I have already mentioned, Berg did have a guilty secret, namely his—may I call it— nominal part in passing information to a foreign power. There's been a good deal of talk about espionage as the background to this case, but I would ask you not to lose sight of the part actually played by this defendant. It was to pass to a country with which he has strong emotional ties details of false information which a man with an obviously twisted mind—and I am bound to stigmatise the dead man's conduct in that way—had been passing to another power. That was all Berg did, whatever Parsons and other unknown, shadowy figures were up to. In short, *he* was nothing more than a post office, but it is clear, is it not, from this whole seething background that there must have been others with a far stronger motive to murder Parsons than ever Berg had. Indeed, I'm not clear what precise motive has been attributed to my client. In so far as he was involved at all, Parsons and he were on the same side, and nothing to the contrary has been proved.

"In short, members of the jury, the prosecution's case is made up of items of circumstantial evidence, with his lies to the police as the strongest point against him. Well, he not only is going to admit that he lied, as I suggest anyone similarly placed might have lied, but he is also going to admit what the prosecution couldn't otherwise prove beyond reasonable doubt, namely that he was in Starforth Street that fateful Friday night and actually witnessed the murder taking place. Members of the jury, if the prosecution couldn't prove that, why should he admit it unless it were true? I ask you to bear that in mind as he gives his evidence before you."

The jury's attention remained with him to the end and Richard, who had been watching them intently all the while, reckoned that he had given them something to think about. He had pitched it just right and there was no doubt that it had been a thoroughly competent and captivating performance. Richard permitted himself a small glow of pride in his friend's forensic talent. He invariably managed to assume the role of sweet reason, and address a jury as though they were the cricket team of which he happened to be the captain and his client the opening batsman.

Berg now made his way to the witness-box and took the oath on the old testament with his head covered. It soon became apparent that he had not only shaken off the lethargy which had gripped him so much of the time in prison, but that his demeanour as a witness was exactly right. He was lucid in his answers and managed to present the aspect of an ordinary man caught up in a web of diabolical circumstance, part responsibility for which he himself now ruefully admitted.

He described in detail his relationship with Parsons and the role which he was suborned into playing. Under Alan's guiding hand, he went on to describe the events of the Friday evening on which Parsons met his death.

"Did you murder Parsons?" Alan asked earnestly.

"I did not."

"Do you know who did?"

"I could only guess."

"No, don't do that, since your guesses, right or wrong, can't be evidence. Could you describe the man you saw commit the crime?"

"I'm afraid I can't. I was some distance away. It was night time and the whole thing was over before I'd realised what had happened."

"You knew Parsons was due to meet someone that evening?"

"Yes."

"He had told you a name?"

"Yes."

"Was it the name of anyone you knew yourself?"

"No. It wasn't anyone I'd met, though I'd heard the name before."

"From Mr. Parsons?"

"Yes."

"I'm not quite following the relevance of your questions, Mr. Scarby," the judge broke in in a puzzled tone.

"I was seeking to show, my lord, that even though Mr. Berg believed Mr. Parsons was going to meet a named individual that evening, he is unable to say of his own knowledge whether or not he did so meet him."

"Hmm. If I understood the accused right, he has said that he can't give a description of the man he saw with Parsons because he wasn't close enough to obtain one."

"That is so, my lord."

"Then it doesn't help us to speculate on the subject, does it Mr. Scarby?"

"I agree, my lord."

Mr. Justice Harris looked at Alan with his head slightly on one side and the tolerant expression of a chess player who has just called out "check".

Alan wanted to give him a wink in return, but luckily refrained. He turned back to the witness.

"Why did you run away afterwards, Mr. Berg?"

"Because I was very frightened."

"Why did you lie when the police first visited you?"

"For the same reason."

"And why were you frightened?"

"Because I suddenly realised I'd strayed into something and was out of my depth."

"Let me now ask you about the stiletto paper-knife." The usher handed it up to Berg.

"Do you recognise it?"

"Yes, I do."

"Whose is it?"

"Mine."

"When did you last see it?"

"I'm afraid I can't remember the exact date. I would assume it must have been very shortly before my arrest, since I used it most days."

"Where was it normally kept?"

"In the top right-hand drawer of my desk—in a sheath."

Alan sat down and the jury, like a tennis crowd, turned their heads to look at Stephen Green as he rose to cross-examine. He did so for just under an hour, but failed to shake Berg either in the consistency of his replies or in the equanimity of his manner. It could be said that Berg had now come clean and that cross-examination was unable to achieve anything other than to emphasise what he himself had already chosen to admit.

When the lunch adjournment came, Alan and Richard felt more cheerful than they had since the case had landed in their laps.

"I thought he gave a very good account of himself in the witness-box," Alan remarked over the top of a cheese roll.

"So do I. What's more I think the jury were impressed, too."

Alan nodded. "Still we'd better not become too euphoric. . . ."

The first witness of the afternoon was Beth Steen. She was dressed in a smart moss green outfit with a matching hat which, to Richard, resembled one half of a velvet meringue. She had also obviously had a hair-do for the occasion. As she removed her right glove in order to take the oath, she threw Berg a small smile, which didn't go unnoticed by prosecuting counsel.

"There's only one matter about which I want to ask you any questions, Miss Steen," Alan said. "Would you be so good as to look at the paper-knife the usher is about to hand to you?"

She gave it a mere glance before returning her gaze to Alan.

"Do you recognise it?"

"Yes, it's Mr. Berg's."

"Were you present when the police were searching Mr. Berg's office and Miss Parrot, who was then employed by the firm, drew attention to the fact it was missing from its usual place?"

"Yes, I was."

"And when did you next see the paper-knife?"

"It was about two weeks ago."

"That is, since Mr. Berg was committed for trial?"

"Oh, certainly, yes."

"Please tell the court the circumstances in which you found it."

"Well, there'd been one or two searches for it in his office but without success, and then one morning about two weeks ago, I decided to have a really thorough look. I pulled the drawer of the desk, in which Mr. Berg normally kept it, right out and I discovered that there was not only a broad crack in the wood of the bottom of the drawer at the back—I'd noticed that before— but when I put my hand at the back, there was a space between two layers of wood there. It occurred to me that things could drop through the crack in the drawer itself and fall between these two layers."

"So what did you do?"

"With a good deal of difficulty we turned the desk on its front."

"Who's *we*?"

"Mr. Femmer and myself."

"Mr. Femmer was with you the whole time?"

"No, I called him when I'd found out what might have happened."

"Yes, go on, please."

"As I say, we turned the desk on to its front and felt between the layers of wood with a metal rod."

"Yes?"

"And found this paper-knife."

"Are you quite certain it's the one Mr. Berg had always had?"

Beth smiled. "Quite certain. As a matter of fact it was I who gave it to him in the first place. Also it fits the sheath."

Alan resumed his seat and Green rose with an air of slow deliberation.

"How much did you pay for it, Miss Steen?"

"Pay for it?" she echoed, taken aback by the unexpectedness of his first question.

"That's what I asked."

'I think it was about fifteen shillings."

"There's nothing very special about it, is there?"

"No-o."

"It's quite a common type of paper-knife, isn't it?"

"Ye-es."

"Miss Steen, you don't seem very happy with my questions. Is something troubling you?"

"Troubling me?"

"Yes, troubling you?"

"No, nothing."

"Good. Do you remember the name of the shop where you bought it?"

"I'm afraid not."

"Come, Miss Steen, surely you must remember!"

"It was a small stationers near London Wall, but I can't remember more than that I'm afraid."

"When did you buy it?"

"Three years ago last Christmas."

"So it was a Christmas present for Mr. Berg?"

"Yes."

"Can you explain to the jury why it took so long for you to find it?"

"I've already explained, we had searched before—or rather I had—and I simply decided to have one more really thorough look for it."

"You realised that it was very important to find it if you could."

"Certainly."

"But you hadn't thought of making this very thorough search until two weeks ago?"

"As I say, I had made searches before."

"But not thorough ones?"

"Obviously not sufficiently thorough ones," she retorted in a defiant tone.

"What it comes to is this, Miss Steen; for the best part of five weeks, this paper-knife, if your evidence is correct, lay hidden in a recess of Mr. Berg's desk?"

"It must have done."

"And was then conveniently found?"

176

"I don't know what you mean by convenient," she said with some heat.

"Wasn't it convenient?"

"No more convenient than its disappearance was to the police."

"Now, now, Miss Steen," the judge broke in, "you mustn't argue the toss with prosecuting counsel."

"He started it, sir—my lord."

"Behave yourself."

Green had meanwhile sat down.

Patrick Femmer who, like all witnesses waiting to give evidence had remained outside the court-room throughout the trial now replaced Beth Steen in the box.

He looked ill-at-ease and fidgeted nervously with his tie during Alan's preliminary questions. A permanent frown was fixed on his brow, and he cast nervous glances round the court as though he suspected hidden dangers to be lurking behind the panelled walls.

He confirmed that Beth Steen had called him in to the room and that he'd assisted her in finding the paper-knife which he said, after examining it for an unconscionable time, was Berg's.

In view of his apparent nervousness, Alan kept his questions to the minimum.

"You don't seem too certain that it is Mr. Berg's paper-knife?" Green said in a challenging tone.

"Well, it must be."

"Why must it be?"

"Because we found it in his desk."

"Tell me in detail how you came to find it?"

"We turned the desk on its side and Miss Steen fished it out with a walking stick."

"A walking stick?"

"That's right."

"You're sure?"

"I thought it was a walking stick . . . it looked like a walking stick."

"It couldn't have been a metal rod?"

"Yes, it could have been."

"There's very little similarity between a metal rod and a walking stick, is there?"

"Well, you see, I wasn't really paying very much attention."

"Very well," Green said in a silky tone. "Now tell me this! Did you turn the desk on to its side or its front or even its back?"

"Let me think . . ." Femmer said uncomfortably, fingering the knot of his tie for the fiftieth time. "Actually, we tilted it several ways."

"Which way up was it when you found the paper-knife?"

"I don't really recall."

"Is that because you still weren't paying much attention?" Green's tone was sarcastic.

"No, I wasn't taking a lot of notice," he agreed with a sickly half-smile. His forehead glistened damply under the light just over his head, and he gave the impression of a man who was himself on trial.

"Do you know how Mr. Berg acquired the paper-knife?" Green asked relentlessly.

"Miss Steen gave it to him as a birthday present."

Alan jumped to his feet in an endeavour to rescue the witness from further catastrophe.

"That reply must surely be hearsay evidence unless the witness was there when the present was made."

"Were you there?" the judge enquired.

"No. It's what Miss Steen told me."

Richard and Alan, who had been listening to the cross-examination with growing dismay, sat rigid with tension waiting for prosecuting counsel to deliver what each of them feared must come with the inevitability of death itself, namely the final blow in the demolition of their witness's credibility.

For a full half-minute Green stared at the unhappy Femmer in thoughtful appraisal.

"The truth is, Mr. Femmer, is it not," he said at last, "that your evidence is a concoction from beginning to end?"

For several seconds Femmer stood staring stupidly back at him, then with a sudden groan he fell sideways in a dead faint.

20

Half an hour later Richard and Alan were back in Alan's chambers, the judge having adjourned the case over the week-end until Monday morning.

"That unbelievably stupid Steen woman!" Richard said explosively. "How dare she make us a party to perjured evidence! It never occurred to me to doubt her story about finding the paper-knife. She's just about flushed Berg's chances down the pan—and laid herself and Femmer open to proceedings for perjury. Though I'd cheerfully prosecute her for that myself. How dare she do what she has!"

"I know," Alan said glumly. "However, I suppose we'd better think about how we're going to pick up the pieces." He sighed. "The pity is that up till Femmer's appearance I thought the case was running our way very nicely."

"It was too. And to think it should be our own witnesses who've blasted it apart."

There was a confused sound of voices in the passage outside and the door opened to admit Alan's clerk.

"Miss Steen's outside, sir," he announced in an anxious voice. "She insists on speaking to Mr. Monk. She's in a very agitated state and refuses to go, although I said you were in conference."

"You'd better have a word with her, Richard."

With a grim expression, Richard left the room. Beth Steen who was sitting on the edge of a chair outside the clerk's room jumped up as soon as she saw him.

"He did it deliberately," she almost shouted at him. "Femmer, I mean. His breakdown in the witness-box was deliberately contrived. . . ."

The next forty-eight hours were amongst the busiest in Richard's career. Discussion and plan-making had gone on far into Friday night and at half past nine the next morning, he went to his office to await events.

The office was normally shut on a Saturday, and after switching the telephone through to his own room, he went upstairs and paced restlessly about, pausing from time to time to look out on the square which provided the background to his professional life.

Just before ten o'clock he heard a knock on the street door and ran down to open it. With his hand resting on the catch, he hesitated a second to brace himself.

"Good morning, Mr. Femmer," he said gravely. "Let's go up to my room." He led the way back upstairs. "It's good of you to call, but it was important that we should have a talk after what happened in court yesterday. As you'll appreciate, various decisions have to be made before the trial resumes on Monday and Mr. Scarby asked me to get in touch with you as a matter of urgency."

"I quite understand, Mr. Monk. Indeed if you hadn't 'phoned me, I was going to try to get in touch with you." He bit nervously at the side of his mouth. "I suppose it's up to me to say something . . . to explain . . . you may think, to apologise . . . but it's not easy to put into words."

"Perhaps I can make it easier for you," Richard said. "Was the evidence you and Miss Steen gave about the finding of the paper-knife a concoction?"

He hung his head and gave a small nod. "I'm afraid so. I was never keen on it, but Miss Steen persuaded me it was the only way we could save Mr. Berg. She came back from seeing him in prison one time and said we'd got to help him somehow. And then, about two days later, she produced that paper-knife, which she'd just bought, and said how we must say we'd found it hidden in a cavity at the back of the desk. I told her we shouldn't. . . I pointed out the awful risks we were running in making up such a story . . . but she became very overwrought and accused me of thinking only of myself. So in the end, I agreed to support the story she proposed we should tell." He shook his head in grim recollection. "I don't mind telling you, Mr. Monk, that I would never have agreed in a hundred years if I'd had so much as an inkling of the horror I'd experience as I stood in that witness-box, stripped of all my self-respect. It was worse than any nightmare. . . ." He glanced up. "What'll happen now?"

"Once the trial is over, the police will certainly come and interview you about the matter."

"Am I likely to be prosecuted?"

"You could be," Richard replied evenly.

"And does the same go for Miss Steen?"

"Certainly. Have you seen her since leaving court yesterday?"

"No. I don't imagine she'll want to see me ever again," he said dully.

He looked up sharply as the telephone began ringing and watched Richard answer it. His expression grew more and more suspicious as Richard held the receiver right against his ear and stared fixedly at the wall, uttering only an occasional monosyllable.

As soon as he had put down the 'phone, Femmer said, "Who was that?"

"A client."

"I asked who?" His voice was suddenly harsh.

"That's none of your business," Richard replied in a tense voice.

"On the contrary, I very much suspect that's precisely what it is. It was Beth Steen, wasn't it?" As he spoke he jumped up from his chair and moved quickly over to the door.

"Where are you going?" Richard asked. But Femmer never answered, and a few seconds later Richard heard the street door slam. He hurried across to the window in time to see his visitor disappear from view round a corner.

Although vital minutes might be being lost, there was obviously nothing he could do until Beth Steen arrived. Precipitate action now might double the confusion and, moreover, he owed it to himself to be completely satisfied before passing the problem to others. He had to unknot the string which bound the parcel, though others could complete the unwrapping.

Twenty long minutes later he heard a taxi pull up outside and saw Beth Steen alight. He hurried down to let her in. She threw him a triumphant look as he opened the door.

"Is he still here?" she hissed.

"He became suspicious and went. He realised it was you on the 'phone and guessed you must still be at his flat. Did you have trouble in persuading him to leave you there?"

"No. I 'phoned him last night and pretended to be very worried about all that had happened and said I must call round and see him this morning to discuss our position. He told me he was coming to see you at ten—which of course I knew—so I said I had to see him before then. He agreed to my going round there at nine and I was able to persuade him to let me stay in the flat until his return, so that he could tell me what you had said."

"And did you find out anything while he was away?"

For answer, Beth produced a passport. It purported to have been issued by the United Arab Republic and was in the name of Alexander Fanos, a merchant of Alexandria. It bore the photograph of a mournful and swarthy-looking Femmer.

So that's how Fanos came into the story! It was a pity Nathan Berg hadn't been able to be more explicit, though Richard was prepared to accept that he hadn't known any more.

"And this is even more interesting," she said, producing with a flourish a stiletto paper-knife from her handbag. Her voice was vibrant with excitement. "This one really is Mr. Berg's."

"Where did you find it?" Richard enquired cautiously.

"In the same drawer in which I found the passport."

"I see. Yes, I think that does clinch things. . . . I'll 'phone the police straightaway."

21

On Monday morning counsel in the case went to see the judge in his room before the trial resumed, as a result of which, as Mr. Justice Harris explained to the jury, the wholly exceptional course was to be taken of adjourning the case for two weeks. This would enable further vital enquiries to be made. In the meantime, he proposed to release Berg on bail.

It was ten days later that Paul Prentice of the D.P.P.'s office telephoned Richard and told him that the prosecution would not be pressing the matter further.

"You're quite satisfied that my client didn't kill Parsons?"

"Everything points to Femmer having done so."

"Have you found him?"

"No. And personally I doubt whether the police ever will. He's almost certainly out of the country by now."

"And what about Miss Steen? What's going to be done about her admitted perjury?"

"No final decision has been taken yet, but I doubt whether the public interest will require her to be prosecuted, having regard to all the circumstances."

"I hoped you'd say that. After all, she was the heroine of the day."

"Yes, warms the heart, doesn't it, Richard, to think of secretaries ready to commit perjury to protect their bosses!"

After speaking to Prentice, Richard telephoned Mrs. Berg. She was silent for a few seconds after he had given her the news about her husband, and only the sound of her breathing told him that the line had not gone dead.

"Thank you for letting me know, Mr. Monk," she said at length. Then after a further silence: "He certainly owes *you* a considerable debt of gratitude."

"Perhaps he was lucky that I always believed him innocent."

"Yes . . . you and Miss Steen . . . you both did. . . ."

Her tone left him in no doubt as to what her own belief had been. She went on, "Anyway, thank you for 'phoning me. I'm naturally relieved by the news, even though it can't now alter the course of events so far as our marriage is concerned."

She rang off, leaving Richard staring at the telephone. Then he gave a shrug. He had been wondering what, indeed, might have been the result if Berg's secretary had not also believed in her employer's innocence—or rather, if his mistress hadn't believed in her lover's. If her self-denying perjury hadn't set its unwitting trap for Femmer.

That evening Richard had a conference with Alan in chambers.

"They're not going on against Berg," he said.

"So I hear. I saw Stephen Green at lunch and he told me." He grinned at Richard. "You were always convinced he was innocent and you were right. Incidentally, did Prentice tell you the whole story, or as much of it as the police have pieced together?"

"No, he just said that everything pointed to Femmer being the murderer, and he thought it unlikely the police would ever catch him. What is the full story?"

"Apparently, Femmer was the head of a spy network working for Arab interests and Gamel was one of his boys. For some time Parsons had been under suspicion as a double agent and it was known that Berg was one of his contacts. So Femmer obtained a job in Berg's firm simply to try to find out exactly what was going on. Eventually, Femmer was satisfied beyond doubt that Parsons was double, if not treble, crossing them, and Gamel was instructed to bump him off. However, he doesn't appear to have been the cold executioner type and he refused. I suppose he must have realised that his own life wouldn't sell very dearly as a result of his disobedience, and the same night that Parsons was murdered, he took an overdose of sleeping pills. His refusal, however, meant that Femmer had to do his own dirty work. So that Parsons, who was expecting to meet Gamel, was in fact confronted by Femmer, though Berg naturally enough assumed Gamel to be the murderer."

"Supposing Berg had been close enough to have recognised Femmer?"

"I know! Of course, Femmer for his part had no knowledge that his employer was going to be in the vicinity. He must have had some anxious moments when he did learn it. . . ."

"But then very skilfully exploited it."

"Quite. It was only after the murder that he removed the paper-knife, so that its disappearance would throw additional suspicion on to Berg. Moreover, he must have kept it for possible further use in that direction. No one was in a better position than Femmer to appreciate that its business end was similar to the actual weapon he did use. Not that I imagine anyone will ever see that again." Alan uncrossed his legs and stretched. "And that's about it. The police are apparently satisfied from all their enquiries that that's the picture, even though they might be hard put to it to prove every detail."

"How did they find out as much as they have?"

"I gather they managed to put the squeeze on some confrère of Gamel's, who opened up to them when he realised that neither discretion nor valour were practical steps." He fell silent for a moment. "What's Berg going to do when it's all over?"

"Go away and hide for a time, if he takes my advice."

"I imagine Miss Steen will go and hide with him?"

"Probably."

A further silence followed. "Well, Richard," Alan said with a mocking grin, "justice triumphs again."

"What's more, I'm ready to start beating you at squash again."

"That certainly has nothing to do with justice."

Richard rose to go. "Incidently, I suppose it was Femmer who made that anonymous 'phone call and tried to frighten me off defending Berg."

"It must have been. Happily, he didn't know his Richard Monk."

"Equally happily, I didn't know all I was in for at the time."

Alan grinned wickedly. "I'm also glad you didn't know what you were in for, or I mightn't have had the opportunity of handling such an interesting case."